GLIMMER OF HOPE

OTHER REALM, BOOK 2

BY HEATHER G HARRIS

DEDICATION

For my Husband, my best friend. Wishing you all the best for all of your future endeavours!

CHAPTER I

I T WAS THE hottest sex I had ever seen. Literally. Steam was pouring off the lovers as they came together; apparently that's what happens when a water elemental and fire elemental get it on. I took a few pictures of the clandestine affair, but the photos weren't all that good. All that atmospheric steam was screwing with getting a decent shot.

Mr Bridges was going to get quite a shock. He had suspected the affair, but not with whom his wife was getting it on. Well, I was assuming he had no idea that his wife had bisexual leanings, but maybe he was fully aware of her inclinations. I expected he'd still be pleased it wasn't his best mate and prime suspect, Greg.

I double-checked that the evidence I had was undeniable, even through the fog, and then I scrambled down the tree and back out of Leanne Symes' garden. Miss Symes was apparently a much closer friend of Mrs Bridges than I'd anticipated. Still, technically I was trespassing, so I didn't want to outstay my welcome.

I was in Cressington, a suburb of Liverpool: lots of

greenery, lots of posh houses and, as it transpired, quite a few affairs. This was my second covert surveillance gig for a cuckolded spouse since I'd moved to Liverpool.

It turns out that Liverpool is the hub of the Other realm, its capital city, if you will. Eight weeks earlier I had accidentally discovered that there are other realms of existence. Along with the Common realm, in which we all exist, there is the Other realm full of magical beings, and the Third realm, which allows you to play with time like it's a Rubik's cube.

I put my childhood home up for sale, and it sold subject to contract within two days; it was in a popular area with no ongoing chain, and it was snapped up at an extraordinary price. There was a lightning-fast transaction, and five weeks later I moved to Liverpool without looking back.

I rented a house on the Wirral and Lord Volderiss lent me some temporary office space as a thank you for saving his son Nate's life. I use the term 'life' loosely; Nate Volderiss is an undead vampyr, so he can't technically be called 'living'.

I haven't been part of the Other realm for long, so I'm still fumbling my way through. I only landed this gig because Lord Volderiss recommended me to one of his security guards, who recommended me to his best mate. Business has been a little slow, but I'd expected that after my relocation. It's still early days.

Following my move to Liverpool, I rebranded my business to Sharp Investigations and Other Services. To make it clear that I'm fully conversant with the Other realm, I've even added cute little triangles to dot the i's because the triangle is its universal symbol. Despite my clear advertisement that I'm good to do all kinds of 'Other' work, clients have hardly been beating a path to my door.

My Common realm work is still trickling in, for which I'm thankful. Tracking down debtors and serving documents is my bread and butter at the moment, which is fine if a little dull, but I hadn't relocated to the Other realm's capital city simply to continue my Common work.

Now that I knew about the Other realm, I spotted discreet triangles everywhere. I could hardly believe I hadn't noticed them before my introduction. I'm a PI, for goodness' sake – I'm supposed to be observant! – but an entire realm had slipped under my radar. It was a little humbling.

I shrugged it off and opened the door to my trusty Ford Focus. Gato, my Great Dane-come-hell hound, was stretched out across the whole of the back seat. 'Hey, puppy,' I greeted him. 'You want to go to the loo?'

He tapped his tail twice to say yes and heaved himself up. I let him out so he could do what he had to. He didn't take long, and he gave me an enthusiastic lick as he climbed back into the car.

I patted him and wiped his slobber off my face. 'Thanks,' I muttered, a touch sarcastically. I'm not sure if he caught the sarcasm. I have no idea how clever hell hounds are, save that Gato is far brighter than a dog and can actually use a human toilet if he feels like it. He can also portal me to any of the realms when necessary – he portals me to the Common every night to recharge my magical batteries ready for a day in the Other. He's cute, loveable and very useful.

I sat in the car and tapped out a quick report to Mr Bridges, complete with photos and my invoice. Some clients prefer to be told the news in person, but he'd asked for a written report. I got that – it was a bit more private, and he didn't have to worry about presenting a socially acceptable front while I told him his wife was cheating on him. I finished the report, spell checked it and pressed send.

I automatically looked at my call log. Still no call from Stone, not one in eight long, lousy weeks. Fuck him. I didn't need him anyway. I tried to pretend the shard of hurt I felt was annoyance, but even *I* wasn't buying that.

I forced myself to dismiss Stone from my mind and pulled up Google maps to navigate my way home. I'm still not familiar with driving around Liverpool; I know the main streets like the back of my hand, but I'd mostly walked or taken buses when I spent my teenage years there. Navigating it in a car is all new. Google told me it would take me forty-five minutes to get home, so I'd probably be there in forty. I'm generally a good driver, but I have a naughty side where speed is concerned.

I was making my way through the city's one-way system when my phone rang. I checked the screen: it was my office number. Lord Volderiss has a rota of receptionists there 24/7; that was one of the perks that had made me accept his offer of office space. Free space, free twenty-four-hour secretary and free security. What's not to like?

I checked the time. It was close to nine p.m. but I didn't have much planned for the evening. 'Jinx,' I answered on my Bluetooth, so I could talk and drive.

'Miss Sharp,' Lord Volderiss's secretary said frostily, 'you have a Mrs Evergreen here to see you.'

It took me a moment to place the name. The only Evergreen I'd met was a dryad, a young mum who had been in Rosie's café when I was introduced to the Other realm.

'Dryad?' I asked.

'Indeed.'

'Okay, I'm five minutes away. Offer her a drink, please, and tell her I'll be with her shortly.' I hung up without waiting for a response. Some of Lord Volderiss's secretaries like me, but Verona doesn't. There was no point wasting my time speaking to someone who made it clear that she considered me beneath her. I was a lowly human while she was a perfect vampyr. All of a vampyr's imperfections get burned out when they change, and they are a stunningly beautiful species.

I haven't told Verona I'm not human yet, mostly because I'm not exactly sure what I really am. Something else, something Other. My main power in any realm is the ability to distinguish if someone is telling the truth or lying. Being a truth seeker is rare even in the Other, so I keep my skills pretty quiet. I've let it be known that I'm a wizard, and I have some skill in the IR, which is a wizard's magic. There are no Latin spells or magic wands, just 'intention' and 'release' – IR. I was wiped out the first few times I used it, but these days it comes pretty easily. So far my limits have been imposed by lack of practice and my imagination; the IR comes easily but not naturally. It isn't my first solution to a problem, but hopefully it will become familiar with time and practice.

I parked in the underground car park at the office and hurried upstairs with Gato at my heels. Joyce Evergreen was sitting in reception looking utterly spent. Her blue eyes no longer looked bright and had dark circles under them, her blonde hair was lank and greasy, and her dark-green skin was several shades paler than it should have been. She was clutching a thin, buff-coloured folder, and her eyes were cast downwards, glazed and unseeing. Joyce was alone, in more ways than one.

When I'd last seen her, she'd had a three-year-old and a baby in tow. I felt a flash of alarm and hoped the kids were all right. She looked up when I walked in, and something like relief filled her eyes. My alarm deepened. I'm a private investigator, not a miracle worker. Whatever was going on, her expectations were high and the trouble was bad.

'Joyce,' I said gently, 'come into my office.'

I guided her to my small office. It had an anteroom where my assistant Hester usually sits and does some typing for me. Hester Sorrell and I have known each other for a couple of months – she was the missing person who catapulted me into discovering the Other realm. It had been a crucible of fire and I felt like we were already fast friends despite the age gap between us. That's a pretty big deal for me because I've been a relatively solitary creature since my parents were murdered. Tonight Hes's desk was empty; she had gone home hours ago.

I led Joyce into my inner sanctum, switching the lights on as I went. My office is sparse and utilitarian. It had a potted plant in one corner that looked fake. It offered some greenery, but apart from that the office is pretty bare. I have a lovely mahogany desk, courtesy of Lord Volderiss, and a matching chair that is equally grand. My two guest chairs are simple wooden ones designed to encourage clients not to linger.

Gato circled three times and settled down on his bed without a fuss. His eyes were forlorn and serious; he knew something bad had happened and it wasn't the time for wagging tails and kisses. He was being a good boy. I'd give him a treat later.

I turned my attention to Joyce and wondered fleetingly if my fake pot plant was offensive to a dryad. I gestured for her to take a chair, and she sank into it without comment. She wasn't carrying a drink, and I wondered if Verona had been petty enough not to offer her one. 'Can I get you anything?' I offered.

Joyce shook her head. When we'd met, she'd been a happy, bright young mum whose sense of humour had really shone through. There was none of that in the woman in front of me.

I sat behind my desk and pulled out my notepad and pen. I often record client conversations if they don't object, but there is still something preferable in making notes by hand. It gives me a focus away from the client's eyes if the subject matter is awkward.

'Do you mind if I record the conversation?' I enquired.

She shook her head again, and I wondered if there was actually going to be a conversation. I pulled out my smartphone and pressed the record app. 'Joyce? When you're ready, tell me how I can help.'

She bit her lip, her eyes still fixed on the floor. 'I don't know if you can help – I don't know if *anyone* can help. Nothing will ever be right again.' She closed her eyes and clenched her jaw. I could almost hear her giving herself a firm talking to. When she opened her eyes, she met my gaze. 'Reggie is dead. My husband is dead. He's been murdered.'

I felt a sharp stab of sympathy, and an echo of the old pain in my heart. I'd lost both my parents when I was eighteen, and I'm familiar with grief and loss. Hell, they're my best friends. Some say that time heals, but trust me, that's bullshit. Time doesn't make it better, nothing does. The loss is there forever, it just becomes part of your existence.

'I'm so sorry,' I said softly.

She nodded. 'Everyone's sorry. They all give me the sympathetic head tilt while they tell me how sorry they are.'

I knew exactly what she meant. I hate the head tilt too, and the emptiness of the platitudes. 'Can you tell me a little more about what happened?'

Her eyes were fierce now. 'They said that it was a robbery, that he got stabbed while he was walking home. But Reggie doesn't walk home, he drives. But our car was in our driveway. I swear to you, he drove to work that day, so it doesn't make sense. None of this makes sense.'

I gave her a moment to see if she would offer more information. She didn't, so I started my questioning as sensitively as I could. 'When did he die?'

'A week ago. On the second of December. Around six p.m., they said. It was dark. He wouldn't walk home in the dark. He grew up street smart, tough, but he wasn't stupid, and he didn't take risks.'

I nodded and waited for her to continue.

'His body...' She started sobbing then wiped angrily at the tears leaking from her eyes. She clenched her jaw and tried again. 'His body was barely recognisable, like he'd been stabbed in a frenzy.' Her voice broke, and she clamped her lips together as she desperately tried to stop herself breaking down. 'The police are investigating, of course, and the Connection too. One of the crossover cops is handling it.'

'Crossover?' I asked, hating my ignorance.

She gave me a watery smile. 'Right, I forgot you're still so new. A crossover is someone that does the same job in both realms, so in this case they're on the Common police force and the Connection. It's Detective Marley.'

I blinked. 'Steve Marley?'

She looked relieved. 'You know him?'

'We went to school together, and we've dealt with each other professionally as well.' I like Steve, and he'd dated a friend of mine in school. We're certainly quite friendly these days, having worked together on a few cases. I trust his instincts – he's a good cop.

'He seems competent but he's busy, and I feel like

he's not invested in getting this sorted. Something about his attitude seems … off, like he thinks Reggie is at fault. I don't know, maybe I'm being too sensitive. All I do know is that the police have decided it's a robbery gone wrong, and that's what they're sticking with. Reggie wouldn't walk home in the dark. He wouldn't. But I have no idea why he was where he was.'

'And you want me to find out what happened?'

She nodded and her eyes fixed fiercely on mine. 'Yes, Jinx. I want you to find who killed my husband. And then I'm going to bring them to justice, one way or another.'

I had experience of the 'other' side of justice. In a moment of kill or be killed, I had killed. It was fresh in my mind and my nightmares.

'Justice,' I agreed, because I knew that if I had the choice to rid the world of my parents' killers, I wouldn't hesitate to make the same decision again.

CHAPTER 2

J OYCE HANDED ME the buff file she was clinging to, but she looked away when I opened it, so I knew the contents were bad.

It was a brief police report together with photographs of the crime scene. I have a pretty strong stomach, but I braced myself before I spread out the pictures. As I looked at them, a chill ran down my spine. Reggie Evergreen had been in the Other when he was attacked and killed. The stabbings were deep, ruthless and frenzied. There was a lot of blood, not just in pools around Reggie but splatters everywhere. The scene ... it was entirely too familiar. It was just like my parents' crime scene. Just like it. My hair stood on end.

I examined the photos closely. The cuts on Reggie were sharp and clean, not jagged or inconsistent in size. They weren't done by a serrated blade. They were *exactly* like the ones on my parents. Both Mum and Dad had cuts in the same place on their bodies – it was one of the reasons I had argued so much with the police when they said it was a botched home invasion. What burglar killed two people in *exactly* the same way?

I took a shallow breath and tried to stay calm. This was a fresh lead after all these years. I'd need to compare it to my parent's crime scene when I could, but from memory … yeah, it had the same hallmarks. My gut was shouting at me and I've learnt never to ignore it.

I tidied up the papers and slipped them back into the folder. I would read the police report when Joyce had gone. 'Can I keep this or would you rather I take a copy?'

She waved it away. 'Keep it. I can't bear the thought of Wren accidentally finding the pictures.'

'How did you get it?' I queried, tapping the folder.

She hesitated then shrugged. 'One of Reggie's best friends is a bit of a wheeler dealer. Ronan Fallows. He's a piper.'

Dammit. 'What's a piper?' I asked, reluctant to reveal my ignorance yet again. Eight weeks in and I still had so much to learn.

'It means he's got an affinity with animals,' she explained. 'Ronan says that he can even *talk* to animals. I think he's teasing, but with Ronan you never know. Anyway, I called him and asked him to get me the file. He has fingers in every pie, particularly where he shouldn't have them. I made a big fuss about it and he promised, probably to shut me up. He got it easily enough, but he was reluctant to give it to me, and when I saw the photos, I realised why. They are all I see when I close my eyes.'

Her eyes filled with tears again, and I hastily passed her a tissue.

I could relate to that. 'Listen to a guided meditation before you sleep,' I suggested. 'It helps me.'

Joyce swiped angrily at her eyes. 'I'm sick of crying, sick of dreaming. Meditation – okay, I'll give it a try.' She blew her nose and took a steadying breath. 'I remember when you were introduced, you told Stone about your parents being killed and that you didn't know who'd done it. You know what I'm going through.'

I nodded but decided against telling her about the similarities in the cases. I didn't want to give her false hope that there might be something more going on than the attack she'd been told about.

'You must have been young when you lost your parents,' Joyce continued. 'I can't bear the not knowing. Please – find out what happened for me, for my children.'

'I'll do my best,' I offered. I learnt early on in my career not to promise more than I can guarantee. I haven't many murder investigations under my belt and I couldn't promise I'd solve this one, but I'd give it my best shot.

'Is Stone still helping you?' she enquired hopefully. I wondered if that was the real reason she'd travelled all this way to meet me. Was she hoping that Stone and I were a package deal?

I shook my head. 'Stone caught a big case a few weeks

ago and I haven't seen him since.' It was the truth – some of it, anyway. I tried pretty hard not to think too much about it.

Joyce was spinning her wedding ring round and round her finger. 'I'm sorry, I haven't even asked about your rates or anything. Reggie was earning decent money and we've got a lot set aside. So as long as it doesn't cost me more than 50,000 pounds to get to the bottom of this, then we're good. I figured that if anyone could find out the truth it would be a truth seeker.'

I quoted her my lowest hourly rate. If this case was linked to my parent's death then I would have happily looked into it for free. If there was a genuine link, I'd give her a rebate.

I opened my top drawer and pulled out my standard investigation contract, filled in the rate and marked on it that I would notify her of costs every 5,000 pounds. I asked if she was willing or able to pay some costs on account, and she wrote me a cheque there and then.

I asked her some more questions as she completed her details on the paperwork. Reggie was an accountant at a firm in Gerrards Cross; he worked in the town centre, and they lived in the suburbs. I know Gerrards Cross well; locally it's referred to as GX, and it isn't far from Beaconsfield, where I'd been born and raised. It is near Rosie's, where Joyce and I first met.

I took copies of Joyce's ID documents and handed

her the contract. She barely scanned it before signing on the dotted line. I promised to get started first thing next morning. Three weeks after leaving the Home Counties, it looked like I was going back again.

I checked Joyce had somewhere to go. Luckily the Travelodge where she was staying is just around the corner from the office, so Gato and I saw her safely to the door. I offered to give her a lift back home the next day but she'd already paid for a train ticket. She said she would be bad company and I accepted her excuse. She needed some headspace and I totally got that.

Gato and I went down to the car park to head home. It was ten p.m. – the evening had come and gone without me. Half an hour later we were home in a village called Bromborough. It has a nice wood for walking Gato and a retail park a five-minute drive away with everything from shoe shops to cinemas. The village itself has a café, a dry cleaners, a funeral parlour and a take-away. Death and Chinese take-out: the village is right up my street.

When we parked on the drive, Hes's car was already there. Gato and I decided to take a brisk walk around the block to stretch our legs before bed, then I'd check in on her.

At this time of night, the tree-lined streets are quiet. It feels like a nice area, and after three weeks I hadn't had any experiences to disabuse me of that notion. If everything goes well and business picks up, I'll probably buy somewhere here. House prices are low in comparison to the Home Counties and with the proceeds from my house sale, I could get a four-bedroom detached in a nice area with change left over for an office space that wasn't rented from a vampyr lord.

When Gato and I got back, I opened the front door and called, 'Hello? Hes, are you still awake?'

'I'm in the living room,' she shouted. 'I made you a cuppa.'

I pulled off my jacket, hung it on the newel post and went in to greet her. The TV was on and Hes was cuddled up in a blanket. She was holding a cup of tea and she looked a little wan; she was having a bad night.

I sat down in the armchair and grabbed a blanket. The house wasn't cold, but there's something homey and comforting about being wrapped up. Gato gave me a brief lick on the hand and left us so he could patrol the house, checking for mice and vampyrs. I turned my focus to Hes.

I picked up my mug of tea and warmed my hands on it. 'Thanks for the cuppa. Did you hear my car pull up?'

'Yeah.' She paused. 'I went to bed in my flat but I heard a weird noise and I totally freaked out, so I drove here.'

'No problem. I gave you a key so you could crash here anytime, you know that.'

Hes smiled gratefully. 'Thanks.' She has mousy-brown hair and an English-rose complexion. She is pretty, but she rarely wears makeup or dresses in racy clothes, although she'd gone through a brief phase of reinvention when she first arrived at university. Then she'd worn makeup and flashy dresses, and changed her name from Hester to Hes. She'd also fallen a little in love with a vampyr, been kidnapped by my next-door neighbour and forced to become Other by getting stabbed in the heart by my magical dagger. So ... yeah, she was done with the reinvention, although the new name had stuck. She'd been remade without her choice or permission, and she is still trying to work out who and what she is. I'd like to say I'm helping her, but I'm equally in the dark about myself.

'Have you heard anything from him?' Hes asked out of the blue.

I blinked, trying to work out which 'him' she was referring to. There were two main contenders: Stone and Nate. I wasn't ready to think about the former, so I assumed she meant the latter.

'Nate? No, sorry, I haven't heard from him for a while.' Nate is the vampyr she's a little in love with. They had a whirlwind romance before she discovered he wasn't human. It's a little hard to reconcile the fact that your true love is actually undead, and even harder to be forgiving when he's drunk your blood. Twice. Not to mention that she'd discovered she was the latest in a long line of human 'beards' for him. It made his declarations of undying love seem a little less genuine and a lot more predatory.

Things between Nate and I are also complicated. I'd saved his life – and then I'd stolen it. I'd become, for want of a better word, his mistress. By using the IR to control him when he was at his weakest, we'd forged a link that unsettled us both.

Soon afterwards Nate left to go to America, hoping that putting hundreds of miles between us would break that link, or at least reduce its efficacy. I don't know exactly where he is, but I always have an itch in my mind. If I focus on it, I know how he is feeling and what he is doing. The whole thing is intrusive for us both, to say the least.

I haven't told anyone about our bond. Nate's father, Lord Volderiss, is the only one who knows about it – that was why he offered me the office in Exchange Flags. There is a slight chance that someone who hurts or kills me might also hurt or kill Nate. It is a worrying concept that I try hard not to think about. And is the flipside also true? If someone drives a stake into Nate's heart, will my heart stop beating too?

'He's messaged a couple of times,' Hes said, staring glumly into her tea. 'I haven't replied.'

'Do you want to?'

'I don't know.' She paused. 'Yes. Probably. I miss

him. We had the best time – it was the best time of my life. And now here I am, stuck in another realm. It's a bit overwhelming.'

I felt sorry for her. Stumbling into another realm hadn't been as shocking for me. I've been a truth seeker my whole life, so I knew something was off about me. Discovering the Other realm was almost a relief because suddenly I wasn't alone any more. I'm not a freak, I'm something *Other*. I even have a cool-sounding title.

'If you miss him, message him back,' I urged.

She sighed. 'But he lied to me about everything.'

'It's either something you can get over or not. If you can get over it, do it. If you can't, let him go.'

'Easier said than done.' She pouted a little, showing her age, all eighteen tender years of it.

I blew on my tea and said nothing. I could do with taking my own advice.

We chatted as we finished our tea. I told her about the steamy elementals, but I didn't mention the Evergreen case; she didn't need any more darkness before she went to sleep to add to the nightmares she still wrestled with.

At midnight we went to bed and Gato sent us both back to the Common for a recharge. I gave him a nod and he obediently followed Hes up to the spare room. She needed his company tonight more than I did. I buried myself under cold sheets and missed the comforting weight of his head on my hip. Sometimes having friends sucks.

I WOKE EARLY to find Gato had joined me sometime in the night. 'Hey, boy. Hes okay?' He gave me a double tap of his tail, which I took as an affirmation. 'Cool.'

I dressed quickly in running clothes and put a flashing collar on Gato. It was still dark and Gato thundering towards someone without warning would scare the shit out of the most stoic of men.

Hes's car had gone from the drive so I guessed she had an early morning lecture to get to. Gato and I started to run. By the time we reached the woods, the light was just starting to kiss the sky. For now, I was in the Common and I wanted to enjoy green grass and blue skies. Later I'd be in the Other and I'd probably stay there for the foreseeable future while I was tracking down Reggie's killer. In this moment, though, I could enjoy the Common sunrises that I've loved for all of my twenty-five years.

Some runs are a struggle, but today's was brisk and effortless. I felt energised and alert as I showered and dressed. Today I was going for business casual: black jeans with a shirt and blazer. They would be comfortable for driving in, but smart enough if I had to interview people. At least, that's what I was aiming for. I swiped my hair into a messy bun, applied some foundation and mascara, and that was me done.

I grabbed a slice of toast and a banana. Gato gave me a baleful stare, and I got the impression he didn't approve. I didn't care; it might not be a healthy breakfast, but it was necessary. He didn't follow me as I grabbed Reggie's file and headed up to the third bedroom.

I'd used the spare room for storage, and there were still a number of boxes in it. It didn't take me long to dig out the one I was looking for: The Murder Box. I always think of it as having capital letters. I'd started it not long after my parents had died, but their death then was still too raw and too close, so I'd put it away. A year later I'd dusted it off and looked at it again. I'd reviewed everything, questioned the police again, and then put it away once more. That pattern was repeated year after year. I couldn't let it go. I won't let their murders go until they were solved.

I opened the box and pulled out the familiar pages of the police report. I was tempted to make a crime wall and put the photographs of my parents' and Reggie's bodies side by side, but I'd done that before and it had haunted me. Far better to look at them with fresh eyes then put them away again for another day. For one thing, I didn't want Hes walking in, seeing them and having a heart attack; for another, I didn't want to lose myself yet again in a desperate, depressive episode that my best friend Lucy would have to shake me out of.

Even after seven years, it still hurts to look at the photos of my parents' crime scene and see them like that. Death robs you of something; once you've seen a dead body, it can't be un-seen. It's taken me years to remember my parents as living people rather than as the dead flesh that I'd found a week after my eighteenth birthday. I took a deep breath and tried to be objective. After all these years, you'd think it would be easier, but whoever said time heals was full of shit.

I opened Reggie's folder and laid his crime scene pictures next to my parents'. The similarities were undeniable; the marks on the bodies were not identical, but near as dammit. I felt a thrill of excitement. It really was a lead. I was almost sure that whoever had killed Reggie had also killed my parents. And this time I was going to find them.

CHAPTER 3

I PACKED MY car quickly, then Gato and I hit the road. I'd already texted Lucy and asked if I could stay at her place in Chalfont St Giles for a few nights, and I'd got a 'hell yeah!' in response, which made me smile. It would be odd going back to the Home Counties and not staying in my childhood home, but I was looking forward to bunking with my bestie for a few nights. Luckily it was only the middle of the working week, so hopefully she wouldn't be too pushy about forcing me to go out and socialise.

I turned on the radio and sang my heart out most of the way. We had one toilet stop, but apart from that we powered through. It had just gone midday when we arrived in Gerrards Cross, we parked up and Gato sent me portalling to the Other. The sky became lilac and the grass became turquoise; I was getting used to it, but it still took a few minutes for my eyes – or my brain – to accept the changes. What made the sky a different colour in the Other? I shook off my musings and focused on the here and now.

I figured that twelve o'clock would be the lunch hour for some of the accountants, so I decided to scout around a bit first. I grabbed a hot sandwich from a café while Gato waited patiently outside for me. When I was full of meatball panini and cappuccino, I bought a sausage roll to go for him. He wolfed it down gratefully then we walked from the accountant's office towards where Reggie's body had been discovered.

Reggie had been found along the side of Packhorse Road. As I was walking down the road, a few things struck me. Firstly, it was pretty busy, and Reggie had supposedly been killed around six p.m. That was rush hour, but the police report said no witnesses had come forward. Gerrards Cross is a relatively posh, upstanding kind of a town, not the type of place where people avert their eyes and hurry on. If he was killed here at that time of day, *someone* had seen it.

The other thing that struck me was the location. Gerrards Cross Common is right next to a small wood, and there's a much shorter path that runs across the Common. Some people might avoid it in the dark, but Reggie was a dryad, and I imagined he'd feel more comfortable among the trees than walking along a busy road. After all, if he was confronted with someone or something scary, all he had to do was run away and submerge himself in a tree.

No, this scene was all kinds of wrong, which meant it

was staged. And that meant his death wasn't a robbery gone wrong – no way, no how. I doubted Reggie had even died here, despite the copious amounts of blood at the crime scene.

On the off-chance that Gato would sniff something out, we meandered to the other end of Gerrards Cross Common and went into the trees. Nothing set him off barking, and nothing made me look twice: no blood splatters or broken branches said 'murder committed here'. Disappointing.

By the time we were done, it was two p.m., which seemed as good a time as any to go knocking on the accountancy firm's door. A quick Google of Wright Freeth and Sykes had told me the firm had been running for nearly thirty years. Reggie wasn't listed in their employees' section. It felt a bit quick off the mark for them to have removed him from their website already, though I supposed a week might be long enough in business terms.

It was cold outside but sunny. Gato sat happily on the pavement to wait for me; he often prefers waiting outside rather than sitting in the car. I gave him a pat and headed in.

The receptionist was bottle-red haired, plump and friendly. She had laughter lines in the corners of her eyes and a ready smile – which froze when I asked to speak to someone about Reggie. She rubbed her eyes. 'This is getting out of hand,' she muttered.

'What is?' I asked.

She hesitated and I put on a little pressure using my truth-seeking instincts. 'No one will know I heard it from you,' I promised.

'Reggie hasn't worked here for well over a year, but he asked us not to tell his wife. He was setting up a consultancy and he knew she'd be anxious about it, so he asked us to keep up the pretence he was working here.' She lowered her voice. 'Joyce has been having a few mental-health problems. I've known Reggie since he started out, and Joyce too. It was such a little thing to do to help him, but it just kept going on. I told him at the end of November that he had to tell Joyce because it had been a year! And now he's dead! And the last thing I did was tell him off!' *All true.*

The receptionist broke down in tears and started to bawl loudly. I patted her awkwardly on the shoulder, reached over and pulled a tissue out of the box on her desk. She took it gratefully and tried to contain her sobbing.

A door opened and a young blond-haired man peered out. He took in the scene and promptly shut his door again. Charming. Another door was opened, this time by an older gentleman. 'Go on,' he said to the receptionist. 'Go home, Amelia. We can manage without you for a couple of hours.'

Amelia made a few token protests but allowed herself to be ushered gently from the building.

When the grey-haired man returned, he apologised. 'I'm sorry about that. Amelia has been under a lot of stress lately. Come into my office so we can have some privacy.' He led me into a spacious, expensive-looking office. I sat down in a chair opposite his desk; it was significantly comfier than my own office chairs, probably designed for clients to remain in as long as they wanted to be charged for.

'I'm sure I added to the poor woman's stress,' I admitted, in case he was thinking about sacking her because of her emotional display. 'I'm investigating the death of Reginald Evergreen.'

'Ah, well. A terrible business.' He sighed then held out his hand. 'I'm Montgomery Freeth. I used to work with Reginald. But I'm still not sure why everyone keeps turning up here.'

I gave his hand a brief shake. 'Jessica Sharp, PI. His wife was under the impression that he still worked here.'

Mr Freeth frowned. 'So I've been told. If I'd known of that deception, I would have put a stop to it. Reginald handed in his notice over a year ago – he said he wanted to start a consultancy business. It was odd because he didn't seem particularly excited about the prospect. I tried to tempt him to stay with a pay raise but he said that money had nothing to do with it. I wished him well and that was it. I occasionally saw him in GX and we exchanged small talk. His new business venture seemed to be going well, and I was glad for him.' *True.*

'When did you last see him?' I asked.

'I can't be sure. A month or two ago at least, in the café around the corner. He was with a friend, so we didn't chat for long.'

'How did he seem?'

Mr Freeth shrugged. 'A little stressed, but who isn't? Running your own business is hard work, and I suspect he was finding that out. Now I'm sorry, but I can't keep repeating the same things time and time again. Please make sure you're the last one Joyce sends.'

'How many others have there been?'

'The police, of course, and the other PI – Elsie something. I have her card here.' He rooted around in his desk drawer and pulled out a business card. It had *Elvira Garcia* and a mobile number written on a plain white card; on the reverse the card was black with the two triangles of the Connection in the top right corner. Dammit. How many Elviras could there be in the Connection?

'Do you mind if I take a note of the number?' I asked with a barely supressed grimace.

'Keep it,' he said. 'She gave her card to the other staff members as well.' He gave a one-shouldered shrug. 'Not that it will do any good. As I said, Reginald hasn't been here for over a year.'

'I presume his desk was cleared out when he left?'

Mr Freeth nodded. 'Yes, quite some time ago. I'm sorry, there's really nothing here. I would help if I could.' *All true.*

I took the card and stuck it in my jeans' pocket. 'Thank you, you've been very helpful. Can I speak to the other members of your staff? Just very briefly.'

He sighed. 'There's been enough disruption, but go on. Briefly.' He gave me a warning look.

I spoke to three other accountants who all expressed sorrow and surprise at Reggie's death but had nothing to contribute. I saved the rude, door-slamming man for last.

He introduced himself as Mr Stannabray. I stretched the truth a little and told him Mr Freeth had wanted him to speak to me. Stannabray explained he had only worked in the company for a month with Mr Evergreen before he'd left. *True.* He barely knew him. *False.*

'You're lying,' I said firmly. 'You knew him.' Gambling a little, I placed Elvira's card face down on his desk so it showed the triangles of the Connection. Elvira's name was hidden, but the symbols of the Connection were there to be seen.

'Damn.' Stannabray sounded annoyed. 'I've already spoken to the other inspector. Look, we hung sometimes in the woods, but just because we're both dryads doesn't mean we were best mates.'

Stannabray was in the Common; he was being rude by not wearing any triangles to indicate that he was of the Other realm. Tut-tut; that was frowned upon. Of course, lying about being in the Connection was also frowned upon, so who was I to throw stones?

'You saw him after he left Wright Freeth and Sykes though, didn't you?'

He shifted in his seat. 'Yeah, I did. That's not a crime, is it?' He was being unhelpful and aggressive. In my experience, that meant he had something to hide.

I could beat around the bush for the next half an hour, or I could compel him to tell me. I hadn't compelled anyone since my own little brush with compulsion, but today the ends justified the means. I needed to find Reggie's killers so I could find my parents' killers. I reached out with my powers and leaned on him. 'What do you not want me to know?' I asked.

He tried to resist it, eyes wide. 'Drugs.' He blurted. 'He hooked me up with someone who sold me drugs.'

'He didn't sell them to you himself?'

'No, he just knew a guy.'

'What's this guy's name?'

'It doesn't matter. He's dead too.'

'Did you tell the inspector this?'

'No. It's nothing to do with Reggie's death.'

'And how do you know that?'

'It was a car accident. Just an accident.'

31

'Tell me his name.'

'Fred Miller.'

'He was Other?'

'Yeah.'

'What was he?'

Stannabray was trying to fight the compulsion. 'A piper,' he said finally. He gave himself a physical and mental shake and freed himself from my magic. He frowned at me, no doubt feeling a bit hazy about what had just happened. 'I'm busy,' he said firmly. 'You've wasted enough of my time. Get out.'

I didn't argue. Compulsions are frowned on a little, and I didn't need him making a scene if he worked out what I had done. I wrote my name and number on the top of his work pad and passed it to him. I couldn't give him my own private investigators business card without it becoming clear that I wasn't part of the Connection, as I'd hinted.

My years as PI have taught me one thing: there is no such thing as a coincidence. Time to dig into poor dead Fred Miller.

CHAPTER 4

I CALLED DETECTIVE Steve Marley, but his mobile rang through to voicemail. I left him a message saying that I'd been hired to look into Reggie Evergreen's death and asked for a face-to-face meeting.

I had discovered that while I was in the Other I could tell whether someone was lying to me even over electronic devices. The downside to that was that I was missing visual cues that would make me continue putting on the pressure, like fidgeting or playing with their hair or looking uncomfortable. It's okay in a pinch, but no replacement for interviewing someone in person.

It was nearly four p.m., time to see if Joyce had made it home. I punched in her address in Google maps and Gato and I headed off. It was only a five-minute drive away – her house was quite close to the centre of town.

Westbury Drive was on a quiet estate; every house looked clean and tidy, the gardens were mowed and windows cleaned. The house in front of me was impressive; a four- or five-bedroomed detached on the outskirts of Greater London. I didn't know about the longevity of

Dryads, but everything in the file suggested that Reggie was only thirty-four years old; his house far surpassed my expectations for someone of that age. Even an accountant.

Gato had a pee then stood by my side. I rang the bell, and Joyce opened the door looking better than she had done the previous day. She was holding Wren in her arms; sometimes family is the best medicine for grief.

She smiled at me. 'Thanks for coming down here so quickly.'

'No problem,' I assured her. 'Can we come in?'

'Of course.' She stepped back and let us in.

Her hallway had a white carpet, so I kicked off my shoes and Gato cleaned his paws carefully on the doormat. 'Good boy,' I praised him, and he gave me a toothy grin.

'I'll just check on Rose and then we'll go into the kitchen,' Joyce suggested.

Rose was sitting quietly on the sofa in the lounge. I greeted with a smile. 'Hi, Rose.'

'Hi, Jinx. Do you like the Other more now?'

'I'm getting there,' I admitted. 'But Common is still a little easier for me.'

Joyce turned on the TV and put on *Peppa Pig*. 'Jinx and I are going to talk in the kitchen for a while, honey. Just call me if you need me.' She set down a beaker of water on the coffee table, ran her hand absently through her daughter's blonde hair and kissed her. Gato sat on the floor next to the child and put his massive head on her lap.

A big smile flashed across Rose's face. 'A hell hound! Cool!' She stroked Gato's head and he closed his eyes in satisfaction. He'd keep an eye on her.

We went into the kitchen. Joyce popped Wren into a Jumperoo so the one-year-old could bounce and gurgle away while we talked. The kitchen was sleek and modern, with black-and-white floor tiles, gleaming white kitchen cupboards and black shiny appliances. Nice.

'Rose seems pretty advanced for her age,' I commented.

'She's always been bright. She's four next week.' Joyce's eyes filled with tears. 'I have no idea how to make her birthday special when her dad has just died. Having a December birthday already sucks a bit, but with this too…'

'Everything is going to suck for a while,' I agreed. 'But you can still make her birthday special.'

'How?'

'Just by being there,' I said simply. 'She needs you more than ever.'

Joyce nodded and rubbed her eyes in frustration. 'I can't stop crying. It's beginning to piss me off. This isn't me. I'm not a sobber. I'm a fixer, but here I am sobbing away.'

'It's only been a week. It takes a while to adjust, to accept. Cut yourself some slack.'

I didn't quite know how to broach the subject of Reggie's fake job, but sometimes beating around the bush helps no one. I decided to go straight to it. 'Reggie quit working for Wright Freeth and Sykes a year ago.'

'I—What? That's not right. I've spoken to Amelia frequently over the last—'

I cut in. 'She lied because Reggie asked her to.'

She blinked. 'Why? That doesn't make any sense.'

'He said you'd been having mental health problems.'

'Mental health problems?' she parroted, disbelief clear in her tone. 'What the hell? Nothing's wrong with my mental health. I had a new baby, I was tired and it was hard work adjusting to having two kids, but that's normal. I didn't have post-natal depression or anything like that. I have no idea what's going on. Why would Reggie say that?' *All true.* She was genuinely bewildered.

'My best guess would be that Reggie wanted Amelia to lie to keep you from learning he'd left his job. Any idea why he'd want to lie about changing jobs?'

She frowned. 'Honestly? No. This is just so weird. We told each other everything – well, I thought we did.'

My phone rang. It was Detective Marley. 'Sorry, Joyce, can I just get this?'

She waved her agreement and I swiped to answer. 'Steve, I'm just with a client.'

'No problem, I'll keep it brief. You're back home?'

'For the next few days, I'd guess.'

'Okay, how about tomorrow morning, 9.30 a.m. at Rosie's? We can have breakfast and talk about Mr Evergreen's case.'

'Sounds good. Bring Mr Fred Miller's case, too.'

There was a beat of silence. 'There is nothing connecting those cases,' he said firmly. *Lie.*

'Let's talk about it tomorrow. Just bring both files. See you.' I rang off before he could protest. I didn't want to get into a discussion over the phone; if Steve Marley was lying to me, I wanted to discuss it in person. Obviously I wasn't planning on compelling him – but I wanted the option. I tucked away my phone. 'Sorry about that.'

'Who is Mr Miller?' Joyce asked.

'Someone else who has died. It looks like a car accident, but it was someone Reggie knew. It will probably come to nothing but it's worth digging into.' I didn't believe that; my gut said it was connected, and so did Steve Marley's reaction.

'I don't know a Mr Miller. How did Reggie know him?'

'I don't know, but he was a piper like Ronan. Maybe Ronan introduced them.'

'Maybe,' she agreed. 'You just missed Ronan. He came by to see if I needed anything.'

'It would be helpful if I could chat to him. Can you

give me his address and phone number?' I asked.

'Sure,' Joyce said. She pulled a pad out of a drawer and scribbled on it, then ripped off the page. 'That's his office address. I'll give him a call to let him know to expect you.'

'I'd rather you didn't,' I said quickly.

Joyce frowned. 'Ronan is Reggie's best friend. He'd never have done anything to Reggie. Honestly, they have a bit of a bromance. It annoyed me endlessly. Reggie frequently chose to hang out with Ronan rather than coming home to his family. But Ronan, he doesn't have a family, so Reggie is it really—' She brought herself up short. '*Was*. Dammit. Reggie *was* Ronan's family.'

As she closed her eyes and blinked away her tears, I remembered my own battle with the present tense. It takes a while to accept your loved one is gone, and your brain and your grammar often refuse to acknowledge it.

Joyce took a deep breath and continued. 'Ronan is a good guy.' *True.*

I nodded but I wanted to form my own view as to what kind of a guy he was. Preconceptions get in the way. Just because Joyce believed he was a good guy didn't mean it was true, just that she *thought* it was true.

I changed the subject to Reggie's background, and Joyce talked about his parents and his sister. They all sounded pretty close. Reggie had grown up dirt poor but in a tight-knit family, and he had stayed in close contact with his older sister.

Reggie was indeed only thirty-four. I questioned Joyce carefully about their finances, alluding to their prosperity at such an early young age. She was proud of Reggie's success and explained that they'd only moved into this house about six months ago. Reggie's life insurance would cover the sizeable mortgage.

Joyce was now a wealthy young woman but, despite that, she wasn't on my suspect list. I'd heard tales of murderers hiring PIs to help them look innocent, and everyone knows it's often the spouse or partner who commits the crime, but that didn't ring true for me in this situation. Joyce didn't know anything about her husband's death – hell, she hadn't known much about his life. Harsh, but true.

After half an hour I excused myself so she could cook dinner. She gave me permission to snoop through the house and I started with Reggie's downstairs office. There was a laptop on the desk, password protected, of course. I dug through the desk drawers. There wasn't much there but it gave an insight into his character: everything was neat and organised, there was a place for everything, and everything was in its place. Reggie was meticulous. His bookshelf ran to accountancy books, investment guides and nature books, no fiction.

I went upstairs to the master bedroom. It was full of all things natural: one wall had tree wallpaper on it, and everything in it was natural woods and fibres. It was painted a soft brown and it felt cosy. I felt intrusive as I rummaged through the bedside tables and wardrobes. They didn't throw up anything of interest, and I ended the search feeling a bit disappointed that there wasn't a little black book full of secrets. But that would have been too easy.

I carried the laptop to Joyce in the kitchen. 'Can I take this?'

She was cooking what looked like Bolognese from scratch. She might be suffering a bereavement, but she was doing her best to keep juggling.

She slid the laptop a sideways glance. 'You can, but I don't know the password. Reggie uses – *used* – Rosebushes1 for all his passwords, and I swear that was the laptop's password too, but I tried it and it didn't work. I tried every permutation I could think of, all lowercase, numbers, no numbers, but no joy. So take it, but if you crack it please keep anything personal on it safe.'

'Of course,' I promised. I have a computer guy. Officially he reconditions old computers, but for me – and for anyone else willing to pay – he'll hack into anything. Rumour has it he's even hacked MI5. Reggie's computer wouldn't be a challenge. 'I'll get out of your hair. I'll be in touch.'

I went into the living room. Gato was on the floor having his tummy stroked by Rose. I smiled at her.

'Thanks for looking after him.'

'I like him. I'd love a hell hound of my own,' she said wistfully.

'Maybe one day you'll get one. I only got Gato a few years ago.' He stood and gave Rose a big slobbery lick, which made her giggle. 'We'll see you soon,' I promised. I called goodbye to Joyce and Wren, and Gato and I let ourselves out.

It was nearing six, so I dropped Lucy a text to say we'd be at her house soon. She replied straight away to say she was already home. Gato and I climbed into the car and I called Hes to give her a quick rundown of the case. She still had a few searches to run for me and said she'd email me the results. She seemed happier today. She'd gone for a run at lunch time and had achieved a personal best. I'd helped get her into running as a kind of physical and mental therapy, and it seemed to be working for her. I rang off and set off to Lucy's.

I didn't need to plug Lucy's address into the sat nav because I knew it so well. I was excited to clock off for the day and see my bestie. It had been weeks since I'd moved to Liverpool and Lucy hadn't been able to visit me yet. I couldn't wait to catch up – although I had to tell her a carefully sanitised version of my life since she could never know of the Other realm.

CHAPTER 5

I'M NOT REALLY the type of girl to scream, but I let out a little shriek of happiness when Lucy opened the front door. She gave a similar squeal of joy and pulled me in for a big hug. Gato was bounding around us, barking happily.

Lucy let me go and gave Gato some attention. 'Hey, boy!' she cooed. 'How are you doing? Did you miss me?' Gato gave her some full body wags and a big lick – he had missed her.

'Ugh, Gato!' she chastened, wiping his drool off her perfectly made-up face. 'Well, there goes the makeup!' she laughed.

'You're beautiful without it,' I assured her. She is: she doesn't need cosmetic help to be beautiful. She has flawless pale skin, light-blonde hair and a warm smile, not to mention a very kind soul. Her inner beauty shines through.

Lucy was adopted when she was three but whatever darkness she had come from has never touched her spirit. Ever since then she's worked hard to be accepted by the people around her. She's a people person – I still find it a bit odd that she's an accountant. Suddenly it occurred to me that she might have known Reggie. Damn. I really hadn't wanted to bring this case home but I'd have to ask. Fingers crossed she hadn't known him.

I grabbed my overnight bag from the car, and we went into Lucy's house. Her home is immaculate, like it's been put together by an interior designer and just been freshly cleaned. Every room is painted in a soft colour and the whole house shares the same colour palette. I always have house envy when I visit. If she ever wants to jack in accountancy, she will definitely have a solid career in revamping people's homes.

Lucy proposed takeout, which I was all for. We both changed into comfier clothes and settled in the lounge with a cuppa.

'How is it going at your new firm?' I asked, sipping my brew.

She brightened. 'It's great! Everyone is so friendly and the work is a lot more interesting. I'm supporting one of the partners on some business accounts, and I've been doing a lot of face to face with clients. I think they're really positive about me too – they've already told me my future will be really bright.'

I was genuinely thrilled for her. If anyone deserves success, it's her. 'That's great, Luce. Well done. I knew you'd smash it.'

She flashed me a brilliant smile. 'Thanks! Enough about me, tell me about what juicy case landed you back down here.'

I grimaced. 'A murder, actually. Reggie Evergreen. I'd met his wife once and she asked me to investigate.'

Lucy's smile vanished. 'I heard about that. So sad. I didn't know Evergreen personally, but he was very well thought of in the industry – until he dropped out a year ago. He was a good accountant and no one quite knows why he took a sabbatical. My boss said he was a rising star. All a bit odd, really. And it's absolutely terrifying that he got stabbed like that just walking home in GX of all places!'

'I know, right? One of the poshest neighbourhoods around.' It was interesting that she thought he was on a sabbatical rather than setting up his own consultancy.

'You virtually have to be a millionaire to live there,' Lucy agreed. 'How on earth did he afford his house?'

'Big mortgage, apparently. All now nicely paid off.'

'I know the wife hired you, but are you looking at her?'

I shook my head. 'No, not really. She's got two kids, a three-year-old and a one-year-old. She has her hands full, and she needed the support of her husband. Besides, she's devastated. No, I don't buy her being involved, but she is pretty clueless about his life. He maintained the fiction that he was still working at Wright Freeth and Sykes, so it was a bit of a shock for her to find he wasn't. I wouldn't tell you about it, but it's going to be all over town now that the firm knows he was pretending still to be there. And they're eager to distance themselves from the murder.'

'Understandably,' Lucy said sympathetically. 'The poor wife.'

I was relieved she didn't know Reggie, and I didn't want to tell her anything about the potential drug lead, so I changed the topic. 'Enough about my work. How is it going with that guy you were seeing? James?'

Lucy gave me a coy smile. 'It's going really well, actually. We've only been on a handful of dates but he's been great. I'm all for women's lib, but there's something so nice about dating someone who treats you well – you know, he holds doors for me, that kind of thing. He's very respectful. He's an old-school gentleman.' She was smiling softly and I could see she was happy. 'I'm enjoying it. No pressure on it going somewhere.' *Lie*. She wanted it to go somewhere.

'You're still young,' I agreed. 'No hurry to settle down.'

She snorted. 'No danger of that, it's only been eight dates or something. But yeah, it's great. Now, how about you and that Zachary Stone.'

My smile dropped and I bought some time by sipping my tea. I couldn't tell her everything because she was

Common, but I had to tell her something so she could understand where I was at. 'I liked him,' I admitted. 'Really liked him. I thought we might have something. Then I found out he'd done something underhand. Basically, he engineered our supposed accidental meet up, and he lied about us having a mutual acquaintance. Our whole relationship was based on a lie.'

Lucy looked at me sympathetically. 'I know how you hate people lying.'

'I hate it, and I hate that he pulled one over me. I'm supposed to be a tough, street-smart PI, and he tricked me.'

'It kicked your self-confidence,' she suggested. 'And your ego.'

I knew she'd understand where I was at. 'Yeah, it did. I thought I could read people so well, but Stone... I thought he was really into me.'

'Maybe he was. The lie was at the beginning when you first met, right? It doesn't follow that everything else was a lie.'

'I know, but I just can't get past it. Anyway, it doesn't matter. When I found out what he'd done, I called him and asked him to ring me back. He never called, not once in eight weeks. I was clearly delusional about what we had. We were only hanging out a few days, and I guess I built it up in my head to be something it wasn't.' I sighed. 'I'm starving. Let's order the pizza.'

Lucy let me change the subject but she sat next to me on the sofa, ostensibly so we could look at the menu together, although I knew it was so she could give me a hug. She's the best.

She rolled her eyes when I picked a margherita, but there's a reason it's the most common choice: it's the best. We switched on the TV and found our favourite show, *Gilmore Girls*. When the pizza arrived, we cracked open a bottle of white wine and spent the rest of the night giggling and reminiscing about good times. It was exactly what I needed.

We called time at 11.30p.m. because Lucy had to be up early for work the next day. She asked me to lock up after myself in the morning and hugged me again in case I didn't get up before she left for the day.

In my room, Gato portalled me to the Common for my nightly recharge. Having a hell hound was incredibly helpful; I had no idea how long I could exist in the Other before being expelled, and I'd never have to find out. A nightly recharge kept me fresh and strong, and so far I'd never felt my magical strength decrease. I had no idea if this was because I was magically strong or because I had the luxury of Gato at my side.

I snuggled into the bed with him next to me. I imagined a beach with the ocean crashing against it and I fell asleep to the sounds of imaginary waves.

LUCY IS AN early bird and she was gone for the day when I woke at 7a.m. Gato sent me to the Other, then we went for a brisk five-kilometre run to get the blood pumping. Afterwards I showered, dressed and fed him. I didn't bother with my own breakfast since I was meeting Detective Marley at Rosie's. I might as well take advantage of a more exciting breakfast. Lucy had sausages, bacon and eggs in her fridge, but it was too much effort for me to cook for myself. Maybe Luce and I could have a fry-up at the weekend if I was still there.

I locked up the house and Gato and I hopped into my car. We were going to be early to Rosie's, but I always prefer to be early rather than late. When we parked, it was clear that the café was doing a good trade; it was just gone 8.45 a.m. and already there was a queue nearly to the door.

Rosie's is a dog-friendly café, the only proviso being that the dog has to be kept on a lead, so I hooked up Gato's collar and we went inside.

It took ten minutes to get to the front of the queue. Roscoe was serving, together with another fire elemental. 'Jinx!' he greeted me enthusiastically. 'It's great to see you. It's busy at the moment, but things will slow down in half an hour or so. I'll pop over a bit later for a chat if you're still here. What can I get you?'

'That'd be great. I'll have a full English and a chai latte. And two sausages for Gato.'

'White or brown toast?'

'White, please. I know it's not as good for me but it's so much tastier.'

'Like most things in life.' He grinned. 'Anything you want to swap out?'

'No thanks, I like it all.'

'Okay. Maxwell will bring over your drink and the food will be about ten minutes.'

'Great, thank you.' I paid with my card and looked around for a seat. There was an empty table at the front of the shop near the window that gave me the opportunity to spot Steve on his way in.

Maxwell, the other fire elemental, brought over my drink. 'Nice to meet you, Jinx.' He smiled. 'Roscoe was pretty excited to be called to your recent ... adventure. I'm sorry I missed it – I was out of town visiting my mum.'

'Next time,' I promised him.

He gave me a thumbs up, then went back to help Roscoe tackle the queue. As he passed, he brushed his hand along Roscoe's shoulders and gave him a warm smile. They were more than co-workers. I sighed; everyone but me seemed capable of finding the yin to their yang.

I turned my chair so I had my back to the wall and

could see outside but could also see the queue. It was fascinating watching people as they surreptitiously shifted from being in the Common, to strolling out in to the Other. Having a portal in your business was a definite advantage. I wondered how Roscoe had come to acquire one.

I passed the next ten minutes trying to guess what kind of Other each person in the queue was. To my surprise, I got it right more often than not. Vampyrs were easy to spot; even in the Common they were drop-dead gorgeous. Dryads just somehow had an earthy feel. I felt a kind of gut recognition for wizards, and trolls were huge even in the Common.

I didn't guess the siren correctly, and I had no idea what the last woman in the queue was. She acquired a triangle as she went into the Other, but nothing else about her appearance changed at all. Her naturally red hair remained fire free, so she wasn't an elemental, and somehow I knew she wasn't a wizard. I didn't know what she was. I stared too long and accidentally met her jade-green gaze. She gave me a slightly superior look as she edged out of the café.

Roscoe brought over my food. I was just finishing eating when Steve came in. He waved to me and joined the queue. He wasn't dressed in uniform, so I figured he deserved some caffeine for coming here and meeting me on his day off. Steve was in the Common as he entered, but when he came back he had the two triangles of the Connection on his forehead.

He paused mid-step when he saw that I had the smallest triangle and the largest triangle on my forehead. The latter was the symbol that I had experienced the Third realm. When I had woken up after the final showdown with Mrs H, the second triangle had disappeared. It was missing because Stone had deputised me into the Connection for the duration of our first case and then I was booted out of the Connection without so much as a *ciao*. Rather like the way Stone had exited my life. Not that I was bitter.

Steve sat opposite me. He took a few moments to find what he wanted to say. 'I always knew something was off about you,' he said finally.

'Cheers,' I said dryly.

'I didn't mean it like that. How come I've never seen you here before?'

'I was hidden,' I admitted. 'I only got introduced a few weeks ago.'

'Well, talk about the deep end. I guess your parents were going to Introduce you when you were a little older. There's a faction that's very keen on that because it can be difficult on the young ones, marching them back and forth through portals all the time. Once you're in the Other, you're in it, and it can be inconvenient at times.'

'I don't know what my parents' thought processes

51

were – they died before we could discuss them. They were inspectors. Did you know?'

He nodded. 'I heard your parents had died just after we left school. When I joined the crossover police and the Connection, I tried to pull the file. Access denied. Eventually I asked a mate with higher clearance to get it for me. He said he would but when he'd looked at it, he refused to hand it over. He told me your parents were inspectors and to leave it alone. I still don't have clearance to look at the file. Sorry.'

Stone had clearance and he'd looked at the file. He'd promised that we would look at it together after Hester's case, but instead he'd done his disappearing act.

'No worries,' I said. 'I really appreciate that you tried.'

Steve nodded and smiled wryly. 'This conversation is going to be very different to what I'd planned. It makes it a lot easier now that you're Other too. We'll start with the easy stuff first. Fred Miller – he was a piper.' He paused, checking my face for understanding.

'Good with animals?' I suggested.

Steve nodded. 'Yeah, but there's a bit more to it than that. Some Other creatures, like selkies, dwarves and unicorns, can be controlled by a piper. As you can imagine, they're not too happy about it. Pipers are a very secretive and insular lot. The pipers' guild has a representative in the Connection but it took a lot of lobbying to get him there. There was a fear that he might try to use his influence to sway votes in a certain way. In the end, the witches agreed to spell the piper for the duration of every symposium meeting, and the piper agreed because it was the only way to get representation.

'Pipers can be very useful because they have a good relationship with farmers and zoos. The majority of them focus their work on Common animals – they are groundkeepers, pest controllers, that kind of thing. A few specialise in magical creatures that aren't sentient – selkies, unicorns and the like. Your piper, Fred Miller, was one of those. That made me look a little closer at his death, and I'm sure he was into something he shouldn't have been. But everything just reads "car accident in the Common". He wasn't even in the Other when he died.'

He leaned forwards. 'I would have kept on believing that if the Connection hadn't sent an inspector. She took over my file on Miller, and now it's classified, as is my file on Reggie Evergreen. The cases are connected, but I don't know how. Luckily I frequently work in my own time at home, so I'd made copies of the files. I don't know why they've been classified, but you can take a look at them.'

Steve pulled out two folders and passed them to me. He ate his breakfast while I pored over the reports. Evergreen's file was the same as the one Joyce had given me, so I discarded it after a cursory glance. Miller's was all new. Not only had he been in a car accident, it had been quite a pile up. Cause of death, projectile through the chest. Jeez: that'd do it.

After I'd had a good look, I passed the folders back to Steve and he put them away.

He continued. 'I'd managed to do some more work on Evergreen The information I found isn't in that file because the case was taken away from me before I had chance to print a more up-to-date copy. But Evergreen was in the Other when he died. The Other medical examiner was confident that the slashes were made from some sort of claw rather than a blade. From the wounds on his body, I'd eliminated wizards, witches, trolls, vampyrs and elves. That means we're looking at dragons, daemons and unicorns.'

'Unicorns? Really?'

'Nasty bastards,' Steve confirmed. 'Instead of hooves they've got clawed feet – think griffin. In fact, griffins should be on the suspect list too.'

Since Steve was sharing, it was only right that I did too. 'One of Evergreen's co-workers brought drugs from Miller.'

Steve leaned forwards. 'Did he now? That makes a little more sense. There must have been a connection between Miller and Evergreen – perhaps Miller sold drugs to Evergreen too. I didn't manage to dig into Miller's financials, but he was doing very well for a piper. I suspect he was doing a little illegal animal piping on the side, but drugs would work as well. That also explains why an inspector would be involved. I've heard there's been a spate of drug-related deaths up in Liverpool and Manchester.'

'What kind of drugs are we talking about?'

'Well now, that's the thing. It's a new drug, focused solely on Others. It's the first of its kind that we know of. This is all hush-hush – it's what I've learnt from talking to some other crossovers in Narcotics. Everyone is trying to keep it quiet, so there have been no bulletins. The drug has different street names: Boost, Eternal Power, Pulse. Apparently, it temporarily boosts your magical powers. More importantly, it significantly extends the time you can stay in the Other.'

'You said there have been drug-related deaths?'

'A few overdoses. That's what I've heard, but as I said, this isn't really my beat. About the only thing that we know for certain is that Boost is made using powdered unicorn horn.'

'I bet the unicorns aren't happy about that,' I offered.

'Probably not, but they grow their horns back. I wouldn't want to try to get near any unicorns to harvest them, though.'

'Do you think the unicorns are part of it?'

He shrugged. 'They're not recognised as sentient, but it's hard to imagine anyone getting a horn off a unicorn without its consent.'

'Fred Miller was a piper…' I pointed out.

Steve ran his hand through his short, greying hair. 'Yes. As I said, the inspector's involvement makes a little more sense now.'

I sighed. 'It's Elvira, isn't it?'

He raised an eyebrow. 'You know Inspector Garcia?'

'Just a little. Lucky me. She's not my biggest fan.'

He grinned. 'But you're so personable!'

I stuck out my tongue.

We talked a little more about Reggie's death, but Steve didn't have any great revelations to impart. He didn't believe the line he'd been fed that it was a robbery gone wrong, but his orders had come down from on high. It was interesting that someone senior was keeping this quiet.

We parted shortly afterwards. As I left, I waved good-bye to Roscoe and Maxwell. The café was still busy, so we hadn't managed to grab time to chat. I'd catch them another time.

I had three strings to pull on next: Ronan, the laptop, and a local miscreant who would know more about the drug scene. What to tackle first? Choices, choices, choices.

CHAPTER 6

IN THE END I decided to drop my laptop off to my tech guy, Mo, on the way to my miscreant. Mo lives in a terraced house in Slough. I knocked loudly but he didn't answer.

I was just heading back to the car when he opened the door with a warm smile. 'Jinx! Long time no see.' He offered me a fist bump, which I returned awkwardly. I'm not really a fist-bump person.

'Hey, Mo, how are you doing?'

He looked good, as always. He's mixed race, though I'm not sure of his heritage – maybe Indian and white British. His skin is tanned, he has short dark hair and dark eyes – and he's built. He looks nothing like a computer geek: no glasses, no spots, no stutter. Mo was in a relationship when we first met and I wondered if he was still hooked up. Stone had no designs on me, so I was free and single, and I needed to remember it.

'Good, thanks. You?' Mo replied.

'Yeah, I'm good. I've relocated to Liverpool.'

He raised an eyebrow. 'Pretty big move.'

'Ready for a change, I guess.' I changed the topic, since I couldn't very well start blathering about vampyrs or elementals. 'Can you get into this laptop for me? The owner has died and I need to take a look.'

'The cops didn't want it?' he asked, surprised.

'Nah. They think the death was a random stabbing so they're not looking into the victim. He lied to his wife about his job for the last year, though, so I need to work out what he was up to.'

Mo took the laptop. 'No problem. I've got a few urgents to work on first but I'll get to this as soon as I can. Usual fee.'

I nodded. 'That's fine. Thanks.' I wanted to make small talk but came up blank. 'Okay. Well, call me.' I waved and hopped back into the car.

'Ugh. "Call me"?' I muttered to myself. Gato gave me a doggy grin from the back seat. He thought I was lame too.

Errand one sorted, I plugged in the address for errand two. I was off to see Archie Samuel, the son of my friend and occasional client, Lord Wilfred Samuel. I dropped a text to Wilf to give him a heads-up that I was on my way. I'd only recently learnt that Wilf was a werewolf – and I had very little idea what that meant.

In the battle of the bombed-out church, the were-wolves had come to help me, or rather help Hes. In wolf form they'd been huge and hulking, far bigger than their human forms allowed for. The night of the battle wasn't a full moon so I guessed that they could shift to wolf form at will, but it was all guesswork and conjecture on my part.

My main guides into the Other realm had been Stone and Nate. Nate isn't a fan of werewolves; there's a history between them and vampyrs that I'm not a party to, so Nate hadn't given me much intel. Stone had been educating me on everything, so his knowledge had been focused on what I immediately needed to know.

Even now, I could feel Nate like an itch in my brain. Involuntarily I focused on the feeling, and I could tell instantly that he was hungry and bored. Damn it. I pulled back from Nate and hoped I hadn't bothered him too much with my accidental intrusion.

I pulled up at Wilf's luxurious digs, an Edwardian build in pristine condition, and rang the doorbell. As ever, the door was opened by a smiling Mrs Dawes. Short, plump and in her fifties, she was always ready with confectionery and a smile. Her hair was in a neat brunette bob, but today she was wearing a swipe of lipstick and she had a triangle on her forehead. Huh. She must be a werewolf too. I would never have guessed that.

She greeted me warmly. 'Good morning, Jinx. Lord Wilfred said to expect you. And who is this handsome pup?' she cooed to Gato, who wagged his tail in response.

'My hound, Gato. Is he okay to come in?'

'Of course. We're friendly with anything canine here.' She laughed as she looked at the triangle on my head then stepped back and held open the door. 'Come on in, my lovelies.'

Mrs Dawes led us to the receiving room, even though I knew the way by now. The room was airy and light with pale yellow walls and numerous mismatched sofas set across from each other. Wilf and Archie were sitting opposite each other but they were smiling and looking far more relaxed than the last time I'd seen them together.

Wilf rose to his feet as I walked in and Archie copied him. As usual, I noted their blond hair and pale skin but this time I couldn't fail to note the solitary triangles on their foreheads. They were in the Other. It surprised me a little that Wilf didn't have the triangle of the Third realm, but annoyingly I couldn't ask him about it; if he didn't know about the Third realm, little old me couldn't be the one to tell him. The Verdict is a pain in the ass.

Wilf air-kissed me hello and Archie gave me a friendly enough nod. He was certainly being much more pleasant than the last time I'd met him. They both held their hands out to Gato who sniffed them obligingly before giving them both a wag of approval then laying down in front of the blazing fire. Gato loves a fire to lie next to.

'Sit, please.' Wilf gestured to one of the sofas and I sat while Mrs Dawes fussed, pouring us all cups of tea and handing out some nice biscuits. It was a little after eleven, so I took one happily. I was about to pass one to Gato when Mrs Dawes offered him some form of bone. He made a happy noise and settled down to gnaw on it.

'Don't worry dear,' she said to me, 'it won't splinter.' I was grateful for the reassurance but, looking at the bone, I couldn't place what animal it had come from. I decided it was best not to ask.

'What can I do for you, Jinx?' asked Wilf expansively.

'Well,' I started, 'I was actually hoping that Archie could help. I'm doing some digging on a new drug in the Other, and I wondered if he might know anything about it. I remember last time we met there was some discussion of drug taking.'

Archie shifted uncomfortably. 'I've been clean for the last six weeks. I'm not sure what help I can offer.' *All true.*

'I'm glad to hear that. Can I ask you a few questions?'

Archie exchanged a look with his dad who gave him an encouraging nod. 'Sure,' he said. 'Why not?'

'Do you have any Other drug contacts that I could speak to?'

'I could give you a name. Most of the time I took Common drugs – cocaine mainly. But one of the guys I know, he did mention something new to me. I said I wasn't interested.' *All true again.* 'I'm not sure if he would speak to you, though. I think it would only work if I rang him and acted interested.' He grimaced a little. He was clean, but he wasn't exactly wanting to burn that bridge. If my deal went sour, his dealer wouldn't be accepting Archie's business again.

'I'm not the police,' I pointed out. 'I'm just a PI, so you're not snitching. I'm looking into a couple of deaths – Fred Miller and Reggie Evergreen. You know either of them?'

Wilf frowned and interjected, 'I knew Miller. We'd had … issues.'

'What kind of issues?' I asked curiously.

Wilf debated answering me. I resisted the urge to compel him. 'Pack business,' he said finally, before deciding to elaborate. 'Miller came across one of my wolves doing a night run at Black Park, just stretching out the kinks. Normally we run in small packs of at least three or four, but this wolf was alone. We use Black Park quite a lot and she felt safe by herself. The park has good wide paths that people stick to, which means we're safe to roam off the beaten track. Any Common spotting us just sees a large dog. Anyway, as soon as Miller saw she was alone, he tried to pipe her. Luckily she had finished her run and was already preparing to transform, so when he started piping she was able to start the change back to human before he had a grip on her. Once we're in human form, the piper's call loses its hold. Miller left when he saw her start to change.'

'How did you find out it was Miller?' I asked.

'My wolf had his scent. We went knocking on a few doors and eventually we made our way to him.' I got the impression that the knocking hadn't been friendly. Wilf was being deliberately vague, but everything he said was true.

'What did Miller say when you questioned him?'

'He tried to claim it was an accident, that he thought she was simply a dog. It was bullshit. He knew what he was doing. I told him not to do it again.'

Archie grinned. 'By smashing up his legs.' Wilf gave him a quelling glance.

'When was this?' I queried. I couldn't imagine the urbane Wilf smashing up eggs, let alone legs.

'A month or so ago,' Wilf confirmed.

I raised an eyebrow. 'His legs weren't still broken when he was in the car accident.' Steve had shown me the police report: cause of death had been a projectile into Miller's chest. The accident had been a messy three-car pile-up. Miller had died straight away. There was nothing in the ME's report about broken legs.

Wilf shrugged. 'I expect he went to the witches or a healing wizard.'

'Who would he go to?'

'No idea,' Wilf said, which was true, but I got the feeling that he wouldn't tell me the truth even if he did know.

'Who do you guys use if you're injured?' I asked nosily.

'A local witch,' Wilf said finally. 'Amber DeLea.'

'Can I speak to her?'

'Maybe,' Wilf replied. 'I'll see if I can set something up.'

Archie was tapping away on his phone. 'My man is free now if you want to us to meet him.'

'There's no time like the present.' I stood up.

Wilf was looking at me with concern. 'Miller wasn't a good person. You watch yourself on this one.'

'And Evergreen?'

Wilf shook his head. 'Never heard of him.'

Archie looked at Gato. 'My man's not a fan of dogs.'

I stared at him. 'You're a werewolf,' I pointed out.

He grinned at me. 'Yeah, but I don't meet him while I'm wolf. Your hound can stay here while we visit Dave.'

Dave the drug dealer. His street name required some work.

I looked at Gato. 'Are you happy to chill here?' He lifted his head from the fireplace and gave me a toothy grin, tapped his tail twice and laid his head down again. He was fine to stay.

Archie let out a rumbling growl, which Gato responded to with a similar sound. Huh. I guessed the canine language was similar enough that they could actually communicate. I looked quizzically at Archie.

'I just said I'd look after you, which he agreed with,' he said.

I rolled my eyes. 'I can look after myself.'

'Sure,' said Archie. 'That's why you got kidnapped and we had to ride to the rescue.'

'You didn't ride to my rescue,' I objected. 'You rode to Hes's rescue. I'd already rescued myself!'

'Sure,' Archie repeated in patronising tone. I glared at him and then at Wilf. 'Your son is annoying,' I grumbled.

Wilf smiled. 'Have fun, kids.'

I glared some more. Great: now I was off to meet Dave the drug dealer with my least favourite miscreant in tow. I sighed. 'Come on, Archie, let's go.'

He grinned. 'I'll drive.'

CHAPTER 7

I T TURNED OUT that Archie had an Audi R8. I wasn't sure exactly how much they cost but I knew it was over 100,000 pounds. It was slate grey, and I had to make a conscious effort not to drool. I'm not a complete petrolhead but I do appreciate cars – and this one was something else.

I was trying to contain the fan-girl reaction but I think Archie caught it because he smirked as he slid into the driver's seat. 'Buckle up, baby,' he said.

I rolled my eyes. 'You're like twelve years old. Don't hit on me.'

'I'm nineteen,' he corrected. 'And you're, what – thirty?'

Thirty! The little reprobate! 'Twenty-five,' I huffed, buckling up and folding my arms across my chest.

'Really? You could use some makeup.'

'You could use a personality transplant,' I sniped back.

'What happened to "the customer's always right"?'

'*You* are not my client,' I pointed out firmly. Thank goodness.

Archibald Samuel thought a lot of himself, and he was his own most ardent fan. I thought he was a spoilt little rich boy, and the car had done little to dispel that.

He drove like a man possessed and I had to bite my lip frequently to stop a shriek coming out as we careened around corners at breakneck speed. Luckily the car had traction and stuck to the road like glue, and Archie clearly knew its limitations well. I did not, however, so I was sweating in all sorts of interesting places.

We came to a stop at Black Park. Archie pulled onto a side road, presumably to save buying a ticket in the car park. The ticket included the car registration so it would be clear evidence to confirm our location here if a drug deal was witnessed and prosecuted. Smart, I admitted grudgingly. Maybe he wasn't just an empty-headed aristocratic werewolf.

We left the car and I followed him down a somewhat boggy path. The December air was cold and I wished I had a hat and some gloves, but luckily the frigid air wasn't too cutting. My favourite leather jacket helped.

The lilac sky was dotted with clouds but they looked light and fluffy so hopefully I wouldn't get drenched. I guessed I could always try using the IR to keep off the rain, but that seemed like a waste of magic when an umbrella would do. The IR wasn't my go-to for solving problems. I grimaced. Maybe I'd get it one day, or maybe it was the result of a late introduction to magic, but I was already set in my own stubborn ways.

Archie led me unerringly through the woods down some paths off the beaten track that were obviously used by deer not humans. It was clear he knew the area well.

'Have you been coming here long?' I asked as we wound our way through the dense vegetation.

'All my life.'

'Were you born a werewolf?'

He looked startled. 'I keep forgetting you're new to this. Yeah, the majority of werewolves are born.'

'But they can be made?'

'In extreme circumstances. Most that try to become wolves don't make it. There has to be a spark of something in you to survive the change, and there's no telling if you've got it until you've survived or died. Changing someone is forbidden under the Verdict, except in emergencies to save their life. They have to be in mortal danger before we're allowed to even attempt it.' He paused then continued. 'Mrs Dawes was made rather than born. She was ill – dying – and Dad saved her.' No wonder Mrs Dawes had a little bit of hero worship going on.

'Before or after she worked for you?'

'After. She'd been our housekeeper for a couple of years. I was young, but I remember Mum and Dad arguing about it. Mum didn't think Mrs D should be changed. She was human before, and her chances of surviving were low. When Dad went against Mum's wishes and changed Mrs D anyway, Mum left. She joined a pack in France.'

The pain on Archie's face was visible; his mother's abandonment still hurt him deeply. I realised then that I'd accidentally leaned on Archie to get him to tell me more than he would have divulged otherwise. Oops. I felt instantly guilty about it and dialled back. I have to be so careful in the Other because my magic pours out if I don't make a real effort to contain it.

I asked another question to steer the conversation away from his heartache. 'And you guys don't just turn toothy at the full moon?'

He laughed. 'No, we can turn whenever we want. It's not instantaneous – you have to gather the intention within you to do the change. You have to tap into the wolf, embrace your more basic urges. Most wolves need a minute or two to prepare. The strongest of us can do it in twenty seconds or so, but the weakest will need five minutes.'

'Cool,' I said, meaning it. I loved learning more about the Other realm; it fascinated me. 'Does it hurt?'

Archie's pale skin warmed. He was cute when he blushed. 'No. Actually, it's quite … er … nice. As I said, wolves are more basic, so there has to be a base reward for changing.' He checked his watch. 'We're on time,' he muttered.

We'd been walking through the woods for at least twenty minutes. Archie had kept up a brisk pace and I was glad now that I didn't have a hat, even though I could have still done with the gloves. I shoved my hands into my pockets and came into contact with something: it felt like Glimmer, the magical dagger I'd used to kill my neighbour, Mrs H. Except that just wasn't possible. Glimmer should have been where I left it, in Liverpool.

I pulled the object out of my pocket and unwrapped the lilac material around it with hands that trembled slightly. Glimmer burst into triumphant song as it was exposed to daylight. I had a moment of total shock – it should be in Volderiss's safe where I'd left it. The dagger was far too long to fit into my pocket, but little things like spatial dimensions didn't seem to bother it. It wanted to be in my pocket so it was, even though it didn't fit. Magic, I guessed.

Glimmer was happy to see me again. Its song was so loud and overwhelming that I couldn't think. 'Shush,' I told it firmly. 'Not now.' I covered it quickly in its fabric, which had come from Mrs H's torn skirt, and the song softened and grew silent. I stared dubiously at my pocket. Glimmer was easily fifteen inches long; would I rip my clothes if I put it back in, or would it just resize itself?

Archie had turned when I spoke aloud to Glimmer and he was staring at the bundle in my hands. 'Is that *Glimmer*?' he asked, incredulously.

'You recognise it?'

'I saw it during the battle. What's it doing here?'

That was a damn good question and one I had no answer to, so I didn't answer it. 'What were *you* doing at the battle?'

'Mostly eating ogres,' he said.

'I didn't realise your dad took you.'

'Yeah.' Archie's chest puffed out with self-importance. 'That was my blooding. I've taken a place in the pack now.'

I put the bundle back in my pocket. It fit. I pulled it back out, stared at the length of it, and then put it away again. It didn't make sense, but it was Other, so I let it go. I focused back on Archie. 'I have no idea what any of that means.'

'Your blooding is your first real hunt with the pack. Once you're blooded, you can take on a new role in the pack. We held a tourney for me and now I'm twelfth in seniority.' He said it with obvious pride.

'You're not like … heir to the pack?'

He snorted. 'No, that's not how a pack works. Just because Dad is the alpha doesn't mean I'm the heir-apparent. Pack positions are earned, and strength is everything. Twelfth is pretty impressive for one as young as me.'

I guessed that might be why something had shifted in the dynamic between him and Wilf. Archie was rightfully in the pack now and finally stepping up to the mark. 'Well then,' I said, 'you're welcome for me calling you to the fight.'

He flashed me a grin. 'Call me again next time. It was fun.'

I wouldn't have called the battle fun and it still haunted my dreams. I'm scrappy and a fighter, but I'm not a warrior. To me, there is nothing amusing or entertaining about death.

Archie checked his watch again. 'Come on, or we'll be late.'

We ploughed on. It wasn't long before we joined a main path and came to the lake. 'There's Dave.' Archie pointed discreetly to a white guy dressed in jeans with dreadlocks spilling out of a red bobble hat that was pulled down low. For some reason I hadn't envisaged drug dealers wearing bobble hats, but the hat's brim nicely hid whether or not he was in the Other.

'Let me do the talking,' Archie ordered.

I nodded but I had no intention of staying silent if something needed asking. I'd let him take lead though, and see where it went.

'Yo, Dave,' Archie greeted his dealer.

'Eagle,' Dave responded. I suppressed a snort of derision at Archie's nickname. They did a man handshake then Dave looked enquiringly towards me. 'And who's the babe?'

I resisted the urge to roll my eyes. Dave couldn't be much older than Archie – maybe he was even younger. Either way, I wasn't his babe.

'This is Jessica,' Archie introduced me. It floored me for a moment because I didn't think he knew my real name.

I flashed a smile at Dave and gave him a finger wave. 'Hey.'

'Righteous. Nice to meet you, babe.'

I gritted my teeth and smiled back.

'I told Jessica I could hook her up with some Boost. I know you said you had some.'

'Yeah, man, but it's steep. It's getting some heat. The price is double what I last quoted you.'

'Double? Aw, come on,' Archie complained, but that didn't stop him digging into his pocket and handing Dave what looked like a ridiculously large roll of cash.

Dave took the cash and it disappeared instantly. No change given, I guessed. He passed Archie a little plastic bag concealed in his palm. They shook hands and the baggie disappeared into Archie's pocket, but not before I'd seen the powder. It was bright, luminous pink.

'Boost is bright pink?' It was hard to believe a supposedly deadly drug was sparkly pink – and I mean sparkly. It shone.

'It's the unicorn horn,' Dave confirmed. 'Apparently it makes it pink and glittery. They tried making it without the horn, but its effects didn't last as long. Even a fingernail of this will help you stay in the Other double the time, and give you a real power boost for at least an hour.'

I revised my opinion of Dave. If he knew something about the manufacturing process, he was more than a small-time dealer. Time to dig in. 'Did you know Fred Miller at all?' I asked. 'He used to supply me.' *Lie.*

Dave nodded. 'Yeah, the Fredster was great. Real shame about the car accident. He was good people. He piped for me a few times like, free of charge, when I had a rat problem. He was supreme.' *True.*

'Was he a part of the manufacturing process?' I asked.

Dave hesitated and I leaned on him a little. 'Sure. He handled the local unicorn herd. Word is they've had to hire some big guns to come in and take over. Rumour has it the bossman isn't happy.'

'Who's the bossman?' I asked.

He shrugged. 'No idea, babe. He doesn't mix with people like me. I'm just a cog. I'm hoping to meet him soon, though.' *True.*

'And Reggie Evergreen? Did you know him?' I queried.

'Sure. The accountant,' Dave said. 'He was good people, too. Shocking what muggers will do. Crime is really going through the roof these days.' He spoke with no sense of irony, and his words all rang true. Dave might be a drug dealer, but everything he'd told me had been the truth as he believed it.

'Yeah,' I said drily. 'Shocking. What did the accountant do?'

Dave blinked at me. 'Like, the accounts, babe.'

Really, it was my fault for asking. 'Sure,' I said. 'You know where I can meet someone about the manufacture of Boost? I've an interested party who wants a large volume.' I leaned on him again.

'You'd have to speak to the office about mass distribution. The main office is, like, the farm shop – Highbridge Farm, near High Wycombe. You can chat to someone there. I'll let them know you're coming.'

Crap. Well, now it was time for me to use the IR. I needed him to forget seeing me so, with some regret, I gathered my intention. I wanted him to remember a simple drug deal with Archie, nothing more. I wanted him to forget meeting me entirely.

'Forget,' I said as I released. I stepped away as Dave's eyes became unfocused and sat on a bench a few yards away as if I were just a regular passer-by.

Archie thanked Dave and carefully pointed him in the right direction to go home. He waited until a rather dazed Dave was gone from the lake before he sat down next to me. 'You didn't have to wipe him,' he accused. 'You wizards are all too quick to meddle with our minds. Dave wouldn't have said anything if I'd asked him not to.'

'Maybe,' I said calmly. 'Maybe not. I'm investigating people who are quite happy to kill. I'm not leaving a trail right back to your door.'

Archie glared a little then stood up. 'Come on, let's go.'

I also stood but instead of following him I went to the kiosk at the other side of the lake and grabbed us both a sandwich. I was hungry. Archie was trailing behind me, so I chucked him a meatball sub. We ate our food in stony silence as we headed back to the car.

Archie's silence was pissed off; mine was regretful. I didn't like the idea of messing with someone's mind, but I had no doubt that these guys were dangerous, really dangerous. Reggie would no doubt agree. I needed to keep Archie out of this, and I needed the bad guys not to know that I was coming. I felt bad for Dave, but he was a drug dealer and I was trying to stop his crew. The ends justified the means.

At least, I hoped they did.

CHAPTER 8

ARCHIE AND I had been driving in uncomfortable silence for the last ten minutes. I wasn't a chatty Cathy but it was five minutes longer than I wanted. 'Eagle?' I finally asked to break the tension.

'Archibald – Bald – Bald Eagle – Eagle,' he muttered.

I laughed. 'Sure, all my nicknames are just as convoluted.'

'How did you get to be called Jinx?' he asked curiously.

I shrugged and didn't answer. He didn't need to know that at the height of my grief and teen angst I'd felt like I was a bad luck charm to all who knew me. I'd cut ties with everyone, even Lucy, for their own protection and for my own. I couldn't take one more loss. Lucy, however, had refused to be cut out. She was a Pitbull.

I focused on the road. 'This isn't the way back to your house.'

'Nope,' Archie confirmed. 'This is the way to Highbridge Farm.'

I glared at him. 'There is no way I'm taking you to

Highbridge Farm!'

'Right,' he agreed easily. 'I'm taking you.'

'This isn't your investigation. This has nothing to do with you.'

Archie shrugged. 'I'm bored. So sue me.'

'These guys won't sue you – they'll kill you.'

'If you rock up, they'll kill you,' he countered. 'I can change to my wolf form and do some snooping for you. That's the safest option.'

I sighed. 'I think they're going to object to a werewolf prowling around.'

Archie grinned. 'They won't see me. Trust me.'

I didn't trust him, not even a little bit, but as he was driving the car and I wasn't his parent, I had very little choice in the matter unless I compelled him. And I really didn't want to do that. I was already skating on thin moral ice as it was.

We agreed we would pose as a young couple looking to kill a few hours at the farm. I regretted that we were in the Other; if we'd been in the Common, the drug dealers wouldn't give us a second glance. The Audi R8 wasn't exactly stealth material either.

We parked up at the farm's office and purchased two ridiculously expensive all-day tickets, which gave us free rein over the farm including Santa's grotto. The receptionist was a dryad. I had to stomp on the urge to ask her if she knew about Reggie but, if Miller was right, of course she did. She might even have played a part in his death. Though looking at how frumpy she was, it seemed unlikely.

Archie was enjoying himself immensely. He even took a selfie of us in the main office. My smile looked more like a grimace than I wanted to admit. I gave myself a talking to, put on my big-girl panties and got into my role. Archie was young, rich and attractive; regardless of the fact that I felt like a cougar, I could do this.

I unzipped my coat jacket and undid a further button of my shirt. Archie's eyes bulged slightly. Ha! 'Gosh it sure is warm, honey,' I cooed as I let my hair out of its tie and gave it a ruffle. The woman behind the desk snickered. It was freezing and she knew my game.

I gave her a fast wink then linked my arm through Archie's. 'Come on. You said you knew how to handle a wild animal – now's your turn to show me you can manage a domesticated one.'

'I can handle anything you care to throw my way,' Archie replied after a beat.

'We'll see,' I replied with what I hoped was a flirtatious smile. It had been a while since I'd tried one, so it may have fallen flat. Flirting is not in my skill set.

The farm was large and sprawling, clearly well-run. Its paths were carefully maintained and they had cutesy signposts pointing to the animals. There were no signs for unicorns – and no signs of them either.

There were a few families out doing some pre-Christmas activities as Archie and I selfied our way around the place, posing and pouting by the horses, goats, pigs and ducks. I climbed gamely on the tractor while Archie took some snaps. There was absolutely nothing about this place that struck a sinister chord. Everything was pristine, but I guess that in itself was a warning sign. I'd been to a fair few farms in my childhood and none had been as immaculate as this. But maybe the owner just had high standards.

The farm was fenced the whole way around. The only break in the exterior fence came close to the forest line where there was a gate. That struck me as odd because there was no road leading to it, no worn paths after it, and it was clean and brand new. Whatever we were looking for, we wanted to go through that gate but maybe not now while the crowds were around to witness us.

It was 4.30 p.m. and the winter night was drawing in. We killed time waiting for the cover of darkness by buying some truly delicious hot chocolate in the café. We wasted an hour while we sat and slurped at our drinks and I carried out a land registry search on my phone. The owner of the land was listed as Karkadun Limited, which seemed a bit of an unusual corporation name for farm owners.

I reviewed the farm plans; sure enough, it was part of a much larger plot of land including the forest that the gate led to. Okay, now I was willing to admit that Archie might be helpful. It looked like we might be doing some sneaking about after all.

We took a few more pictures to maintain our cover. The front reception was closed for admissions and the receptionist was now serving in the café. I saw her raise her eyebrows at me and Archie a few times; we were being obnoxious, but she bought it.

I texted Wilf to let him know that we were still hanging out and we'd be back in the not-too-distant future. It's always good to have someone expecting you back; that way they can raise the alarm if you're unexpectedly kidnapped while snooping around a drug operation. All right, so I'd seen zero evidence of drugs – but the worry was there. Besides, Dave the drug dealer had been telling the truth about the operation being centred here, or at least the truth as he knew it.

That's the problem with being a truth seeker. You can hear if people think they are telling the truth or a lie, but it isn't an absolute. If they're wrong about something, but they think they're telling the truth, it buzzes as true even though it isn't. As a kid, it had taken me quite a few years to wrap my head around that. Some would say it taught me cynicism far too young.

I tapped out a quick email update to Joyce, nothing too specific but a reassurance that I was following up a lead, then Archie and I ostensibly left the farm. We drove to the other side of the forest, the extent of the farm's acreage, parked up in a layby and set off into the forest on foot. The forest boundary was fenced; that in itself was unusual.

I zipped up my leather jacket and re-tied my hair in a bun. I checked in my pocket and for some reason felt reassured that Glimmer was there. We climbed over the fence and headed into the darkness.

'Um,' I whispered to Archie, 'when you're wolfy, how wolfy do you get? I mean, are you fully in control, or am I going to have to hide from your wolfiness by climbing up a tree?'

Archie's white teeth flashed in the darkness; I was amusing him. 'Babe, no tree will hide you from me.'

I rolled my eyes, but he probably couldn't see me in the darkness.

'I saw that,' he said. 'Wolves have good night vision. In answer to your question, when I'm wolf I have all the instincts and urges of a wolf, and it takes me a few minutes to get a hold of them. After that, I have to work hard to keep control over the wolf and my urges. So I might want to make an easy meal out of you, but I won't. My human mind has override.'

That wasn't as reassuring as he might have intended.

'Just give me a moment once I've changed and don't make any sudden movements while the change is raw,' he continued. 'I'm gathering my intention now. Shush and give me a minute.'

I swallowed hard and nodded. Sometimes life before I discovered the Other realm seemed boring but tonight wasn't one of those times. Tonight, life pre-realms sounded pretty cosy. Pre-realms I wouldn't have been out in the pitch dark with a werewolf trying to find a herd of angry unicorns. These days, life was weird.

Archie started taking off his clothes. 'What are you doing?' I hissed.

'I'm not getting my clothes ruined. These jeans cost 400 pounds.'

'That's a ridiculous amount of money to spend on jeans,' I griped.

He shrugged. 'Gotta look the part, babe. Now shush.'

'Don't call me babe!' I ground out, whirling around so I couldn't see his naked form. After a few seconds I realised that was a bad idea as I wouldn't know when he'd completed the change and I could move again. I turned around – only to see that he had already changed, and he had caught my sudden movement. Uh-oh.

His eyes were yellow and shone in the dark. His head snapped towards me and I froze. Oh man, this was a pants'-peeing moment if ever there was one. He was the size of a small pony; I had no idea how that was possible because, as a human, he was relatively scrawny. His fur was grey and white with the odd bit of black. He was breathtakingly beautiful and, if it hadn't been for the bared teeth, I'd have wanted to pet him. I have a thing for large canines. Gato, however, had never exhibited the urge to eat me. I stayed very, very still and waited for a sign that Archie was fully in charge.

He was scenting the air and growling low in his throat as he slunk towards me, and I wished I had unwrapped Glimmer. Then he stopped about a metre from me and the growl died abruptly. The teeth disappeared and he gave me an enthusiastic tail wag. I wondered if he could hear the hammering of my heart.

'Glad to have you back with me,' I said as coolly as I could. 'Lead the way, Diefenbaker.' He looked at me blankly; I guess he was too young to have watched *Due South* as a kid.

I grabbed his jeans from the ground and pulled out his car keys. It didn't seem prudent to leave the car keys lying around. As a wolf I was sure he could scent them, but it seemed a silly risk to take. I folded his jeans up and put them on the ground with the rest of his clothes. I pocketed his car keys.

Archie turned on his tail and plunged quickly into the darkness. 'Hey!' I hissed. 'Slowly for the stupid human, remember?'

He eased his pace to a slower trot but I still had to hurry to catch up. My eyes adjusted to the dark but the terrain was uneven and the cover of the trees made the place darker still. I couldn't afford torch light giving me away, so I stumbled along.

Suddenly I had an idea. I needed to see well in the dark to follow the path. I gathered my intention. 'Night vision,' I whispered.

It was like someone had turned on a light: suddenly the path was clear before me.

I felt the tug of my magic letting me know it was being constantly drained to allow for this particular piece of enchantment but I wasn't too worried. I'd recharged last night and I should be good for a while yet. Besides, it wasn't quite daylight but it wasn't far off. Cool.

The IR was growing on me; now I just had to keep remembering that I could use it.

Archie and I picked up the pace now I could see more easily. I broke into a light jog, trying to keep my footfalls quiet. After a few minutes Archie turned towards me and growled. He wasn't as easy to understand as Gato. 'We should have worked out signals beforehand,' I sighed. Hindsight is always 20/20.

I took another step forwards and Archie advanced on me, growling a little louder. 'Right, okay. I'll just stay here, shall I?'

Archie stopped growling and turned back to the forest. He plunged deeper into the trees and in seconds was gone from my sight. Man, he could move. Or perhaps I should say wolf.

Surveillance is a lot more fun when you're in a warm

car with music and snacks. Now I'd stopped moving, the night chill was getting to me and I started to shiver. I didn't dare move, though.

It felt like forever but it was only about ten minutes before Archie came back. He trotted up to me, turned around and led me deeper into the woods. This time it was clear he knew where he was going; there was no stopping and starting as he scented the air, he just ran on confidently with me crashing behind like a troll. Though in fairness, trolls are surprisingly nimble given their bulk.

Archie led me unerringly to a clearing surrounded by another fence. This one was significantly more heavy duty with razor wire on the top. It had a sign that warned of electrocution. I crept closer without touching it while Archie prowled around the perimeter.

I squinted through the gaps in the mesh wire. Bingo: unicorns. There was a herd of about twenty. At first glance, some of them looked like horses because their horns had been shorn off but on closer inspection there were more differences. For starters, the unicorns' eyes were red – glowing, sinister red. Their coats were brilliant white, though, so perhaps they were just albino. There's no need to ascribe evil to a creature just because of the colour of their eyes, right? Besides, Gato's eyes are red sometimes and he's a cutie pie.

Stone had said unicorns were nasty bastards and they were on the list of non-sentient animals that pipers were allowed to control. For all I knew, they could be malicious or they could be just another animal with all of the base urges that come with the territory.

The area they were confined in was criminally small. One of the unicorns near the fence pawed at the ground and whinnied in frustration. My eyes widened as I saw the claws on the end of its leg. This was no horse-like hoof but a wicked bird-like foot with three claws, something like a T-rex would have had. And it had four of them. Damn, I wouldn't want to be kicked by that; a horse could break a rib, but I reckoned a unicorn could disembowel you without even trying.

One of the other unicorns whickered. This one was much smaller, a foal. There were baby unicorns here too. My sense of injustice and outrage roared. This wasn't right; not only were they treating these poor animals inhumanely, they were cutting off parts of their body for use in drug manufacturing. No, just *no*.

I had to do something. I didn't have the power to stop the drug ring, but perhaps I could put a crimp in their manufacturing process. I gathered my intention and directed my energy to the tall gate. 'Open,' I whispered. Nothing happened. Huh.

I gathered my intention again. I needed to let them out; I needed the gate to swing open. 'Open,' I said again, louder this time. Nothing.

This had only happened to me once before, when Mrs

H had created a magical shield, so I guessed this fence was more than electrified. I didn't know enough about the IR to circumvent a shield, if that's what it was, and I was annoyed by my ignorance. I'd have to rectify that when I could – maybe I could go on a course or something: IR for Ignorant Commoners.

I bit my lip. Maybe the electrocution sign was bogus; a lot of farmers used these signs as a deterrent even when the fences weren't electrified, and I couldn't see any kind of power source or generator. I reached out with the back of my hand and cautiously touched it. If an electrical current was present, my hand would curl *away* from the fence.

No zing. No thing. Nothing happened. I swallowed hard. There was one more thing to try, though it was probably a very bad idea. I reached into my pocket and drew out Glimmer. As I unwrapped it, it sang joyfully into the recesses of my mind. 'Oh hush,' I muttered. 'You're just a dagger for now.'

But Glimmer is more than a dagger and I shouldn't have forgotten. As I touched it to the chain-link fence, my arm moved without my conscious thought or control. Before I knew it, I'd cut a huge hole. I had intended to make just a small hole so that the unicorns would have to make it bigger with their claws, giving me time to make tracks, but Glimmer had other ideas.

I gaped at the seven-foot gap in the fence. With my

height and reach, how could I possibly have made that? Then I tabled all thought because the unicorns had noticed the hole and were heading towards it. Towards me.

Archie gave a sharp bark. I didn't need an animal translator to know he was saying, 'What the hell have you done?'

It was time to haul ass. I turned around and started to run, thankful for the night vision that enabled me to move pretty much flat out. The trees, dips and divots slowed me down, but I was giving it my best shot. Nevertheless, I could hear the pounding of clawed feet behind me. At least, I *thought* it was their feet; it might well have been my heart.

'I freed you!' I shouted while I ran. 'I'm the good guy!'

The unicorns either didn't speak English, or they didn't care. I guess they didn't have a whole lot of love for humans after they'd been repeatedly mutilated. I couldn't really blame them but I wished they'd get the memo that I was on Team Unicorn.

Adrenalin was pulsing through me as I pounded through the forest. I heard a whinny behind me, much too close. It came from the fastest member of the herd that was literally right next to me. I dived to my left and felt a burn in my right calf as something struck me. I ran on, trying to dodge left and right; unfortunately, that also meant that I didn't have as much forward motion. The noise of the four-legged horde was growing. They were gaining on me with every moment.

Through my panic, I realised that I could feel Nate reaching out to me. He could undoubtedly feel the fear and pain that were racking me. I didn't have time to focus on our vampyric bond, and I couldn't find the mental wherewithal to reassure him; all I could do was run.

Thank goodness for my morning five-kilometre runs; because of those, I was fit and I had the stamina to keep going. Even with a horde of demon horses on my heels, I could keep running until I ran out of ground. Nothing was going to make me stop because they would kill me if they caught up with me.

The trees and uneven terrain had saved me so far. I hurtled over a ditch and suddenly Archie was there. He leapt over a fallen tree and skidded to a halt in front of me. Before I had time to register his intention, he closed his mouth over my left forearm and threw me onto his back. I gasped as his razor-sharp teeth sliced through my jacket and into my flesh, then I tried my best to cling onto his fur as he turned and started running again.

I leant forwards on him and tucked up my legs. He was the size of a Shetland pony, but I'm pretty sure only kids ride Shetland ponies. It was taking a lot of effort to keep my legs up high and my right calf was burning, although oddly it was not too painful. I wondered, through the haze of panic, if unicorn claws had poison in them. They certainly weren't clean and sanitary.

Archie ran faster, so much faster than I could have run, and faster than the unicorns. They were still chasing us, but he was slowly drawing away. My right arm was throbbing and bleeding and my right calf felt hot, though I didn't feel any pain. God bless adrenaline.

I did a double take as we whirled past Archie's neatly folded clothes, but he didn't stop for them. I guess 400 pound jeans weren't worth his life. Moments later we were at the fence that edged the farm, and he leapt over it without any effort. I clung to him so tightly that my fingers started to feel numb.

Archie skidded to a stop next to his Audi R8 and barked at me. I slid off his back, reached into my pocket and fumbled for the car key. I unlocked the car with trembling hands and opened the passenger door for him. We didn't have time for him to change to human.

I ran around the car and climbed into the driver's seat, turned on the engine and put my foot to the floor. The car leapt forward with a roar and I drove with my heart in my throat.

As I looked in the rear-view mirror, the road behind me exploded with unicorns. Luckily, they seemed uninterested in the car and they crossed the road, flowing into the woods on the other side. Probably, when my heart stopped trying to beat out of my chest, I'd realise that I'd been monumentally stupid.

CHAPTER 9

I DROVE THE car with shaking hands. I reached out to Nate with my mind, touching that part of my head that always itches with the feel of something alien. *I'm okay*, I tried to convey. I felt an answering pulse of relief and then Nate receded from my consciousness. I was grateful for it. Two's a crowd when it's in your head.

I took a few steadying breaths. After five minutes, when I was certain we were far enough away, I pulled over. I dug Elvira's card out of my pocket with stiff fingers that didn't want to co-operate.

I put my phone on number withheld and dialled. It rang twice before she answered. 'Inspector Garcia?'

I lowered my voice in an effort to disguise it. She'd only met me twice, so I hoped it would work. 'A herd of unicorns was being held at Highbridge Farm, High Wycombe. Their horns are used in the manufacture of Boost. Someone set them loose.' I grimaced. I sounded like I was a boy hitting puberty, cracking voice and all.

'Some idiot set a herd of unicorns loose?' Elvira asked incredulously.

'A concerned citizen,' I corrected cattily. 'Twenty unicorns or so.' I read her the address of the farm. 'Tick-tock, inspector. Tick-tock.' I hung up.

Archie Wolf was looking at me balefully. 'What? She'll make sure that no one's hurt and get the unicorns relocated?'

If she got to them before the drug dealers got to them. Hopefully I'd pissed her off sufficiently that she'd hurry in an attempt to find her pubescent tipster.

I checked the time: 6.31 p.m. How could it possibly only be 6.30? It felt like midnight to me. Crap, poor Lucy would be expecting me. I dropped her a quick text. *Got a live lead, don't wait up for me, sorry! J x*

I put my phone away and started the car to drive us back to Wilf's mansion. As I drove, the adrenaline started to leave my system. I felt exhausted, shocked and hurt. Very, very hurt. My calf screamed every time I used the brake or the accelerator. My forearm throbbed and thrummed as I held onto the steering wheel at ten to two. Now I was out of danger, I hoped like hell that a single bite from a werewolf wasn't enough to turn you. I had enough going on in my Other arsenal. I didn't want to start baying at the moon too.

The wolf next to me stilled unnaturally. A beat later, a very naked Archie was sitting there instead. I kept my eyes firmly on the road. 'Cover yourself up,' I instructed. I wasn't a prude, but it was still a little distracting. I bit my lip, worrying about what would happen if the police stopped us. Archie obediently covered himself with his hands. He shot me a sidelong glance but didn't say anything. He was all out of witty repartee; maybe I wasn't the only one battling shock.

I chose the back roads to make sure we didn't pull alongside anyone at traffic lights. It took us longer to make it back to the Samuel mansion, but it was probably the sensible choice. That said, I was conscious that I was still losing blood. The cream interior of the car was ruined red. I couldn't help but think that cream was a bad interior choice for a werewolf.

We parked on the gravel driveway and hopped out. Archie was wholly comfortable in his own skin. Changing naked regularly in front of your pack would do that for you. I admired it really; I'm body confident to a degree but not body brash like he was. Nonetheless, I kept my eyes on the front door while we waited to be admitted.

As usual, Mrs Dawes opened the door with a welcoming smile. She took in my wrecked and bloody clothes and Archie's nudity without that smile faltering. She didn't even blink. 'You two look like you could do with a cookie,' she observed, stepping back to let us in.

'A cookie, a bandage, whichever you find first,' I suggested drily.

'You'll need more than a bandage for those, lovey. I'll ring Amber.'

Amber DeLea was the pack's healing witch. I appreciated Mrs Dawes' thought but I wasn't sure if Wilf would want to bother Amber for little old me. 'I'm not sure that Wilf would approve of that,' I said calmly.

'What wouldn't Wilf approve of?' Wilf called from the sitting room. I followed his voice into the room and silence descended as he took in my hobble and bloodied arm.

'Calling the witch,' I explained.

Wilf gave Archie a hard look. 'You had one outing with Jinx – *one* – and you bring her back damaged?' It sounded to me like he was complaining that Archie had dinged his favourite car.

'He saved me really,' I admitted grudgingly.

Wilf nodded at Mrs Dawes and she stepped out of the room, presumably to call Amber.

Gato stood up from his place on the floor, stretched and stalked towards me. He whined as he sniffed my ruined calf, then turned his great head to Archie and let out a growl of unhappiness.

Archie flinched a little. 'I did save her,' he protested.

Gato held his gaze until Archie looked away. My hound wasn't impressed.

Archie stayed on the other side of the room, as far away from Gato as he could get. I didn't blame him because Gato was using his angriest growl. I stroked and kissed him. 'Hush now, it's just a scratch.' *Lie.*

Gato's eyes narrowed like he had my lie-detecting skills too, but he stopped his rumbling growl.

I sat on the sofa, careful to keep my calf away from the upholstery, and cradled my aching arm across my body. The adrenaline was all but gone; what was left was a lot of pain and a fair amount of shaking. Using Glimmer on the fence had been a mistake, one I wouldn't repeat in a hurry. The dagger had a mind of its own. Literally.

Gato lay down next to me and placed his big head on my lap. As he let out a sorrowful whine, I stroked him. 'I'll be fine,' I said, not sure if I was reassuring him or myself. But my statement didn't buzz with a lie, so that made me feel better.

Mrs Dawes came in with a plate of cookies and a large pot of tea. We were British, so tea would solve anything. 'Amber is half an hour away. Have this to fortify you, then I'll help you clean those wounds.'

I grimaced. I didn't want anyone to clean my wounds because it was going to hurt. I consider myself fairly robust in most ways but having a high pain threshold isn't one of them. I'd had the chance to look at my left calf and it was horrifying. Huge chunks of tissue and muscle had been torn away, and not in a clean way. I had no idea how I'd continued to run, let alone drive. Luckily I'd managed somehow, or else I'd be dead. That was a sobering thought.

I made quick work of the hot drink and the cookie, and they helped with the shock. Mrs Dawes took me to a bathroom and stripped me down. Gato came too; he wasn't willing to let me out of his sight. I appreciated the emotional support, although I wouldn't have admitted that I needed it – not aloud, anyway.

I showered perfunctorily, trying not to moan too loudly as the water hit my wounds. Man, it hurt like a bitch. The water was still draining away pink but the wound was clean enough now.

After I got out, Mrs Dawes helped clean the cuts and applied some good old antibacterial cream. It seemed a little ineffectual, but I appreciated the thought. She gave me fresh underwear and a nightdress so Amber would have easy access to my injuries. The nightdress was a little on the frumpy side but, despite the lace ruffles around the neck and the floral design, I was grateful to her for lending me her clothing. She's a good egg.

Archie's bite mark on my arm was relatively shallow and didn't look too bad now it was clean. Even in the heat of the moment, he'd clearly been careful with his jaws. Away from Archie and Wilf, I felt like I could ask what might be a stupid question. 'Will I turn into a werewolf now?'

Mrs Dawes gave me a quick, one-armed hug. 'Oh, bless you, Jinx! No, lovey. It takes a lot more than a little nibble to turn. To be precise, it takes near-death ravaging.

It's not a pleasant experience.' She hugged me again. 'You'll be right as rain by the time Amber is done with you. There won't be even a mark to show for it all, I promise. Lord Wilfred wouldn't let you be marked by his son's impetuousness.'

'It was my impetuousness that got us into trouble this time,' I admitted.

'I'm sure you had your reasons.' She gave me a trusting smile. My gut liked Mrs Dawes a lot; she was warm and kind, and I frequently got the feeling that she half-wanted to adopt me. I loved her mothering. Now my own mother was gone, no one mothered me anymore. If Mrs Dawes was inclined to coddle me, I was inclined to let her. Just this once. After all, when you're hurt you always want your mum. At that moment, I'd have given my unblemished right arm for my own mum to spend five minutes with me.

The grief rushed up and kicked me in the gut. I closed my eyes against it, fighting the sting that still pissed me off. Surely I had cried enough? I swallowed hard and smiled at Mrs Dawes, clinging to my composure. She smiled back and stroked my shoulder. Tears welled up in my eyes, and I fought them back.

Luckily the moment was broken by the ringing of the doorbell. With one last squeeze, Mrs Dawes bustled off to answer it and I made my way back into the sitting room.

Archie was looking a bit disgruntled. I guess he'd

been told off by Wilf.

'He did save me,' I pointed out quietly.

'He put you in danger first.' Wilf's voice was hard.

'The danger was mostly self-inflicted,' I admitted honestly.

'Neither of you should have gone to the farm. You should have come back here and a trained team from my pack could have carried out a reconnaissance. Instead, you let loose a herd of unicorns. You'd both better hope no one gets killed before they're tracked down.'

'I called Elvira,' I protested. 'I told her the road name. She'll make sure they're relocated safely.'

Wilf nodded and the tension suddenly drained out of him. 'You called the Connection. Good, they can clean up this mess. But that's it for you two – no more gallivanting by yourselves.'

I smiled in my best non-committal way. I like Wilf, but he wasn't my client on this case and he wasn't going to dictate my actions. I wasn't going to piss him off, however. Sometimes, keeping quiet is the best answer. My mum used to say that if you haven't got anything nice to say, don't say anything at all. I try to live by that adage but snarkiness does slip out occasionally, despite my best intentions.

Once again Mrs Dawes came to the rescue as she showed in Amber DeLea. I blinked at her – she was the redhead I'd seen at Rosie's. I guess that answered my question: she was a witch. She was dressed in a black, full-length skirt and a jewel-green top that made her pale skin pop. She had a large leather bag slung over her shoulder.

Amber nodded hello at me and I saw the gleam of recognition in her eyes. She remembered me, too – I must have made an impression. That was a bit galling since I was generally trying to stay off the radar. I knew I'd stared too long when I saw her in the café.

I gave her a little wave. 'Hi, I'm Jinx. My honour to meet you.'

'Amber DeLea,' she responded, touching her hand to her heart and bowing. 'My honour to meet you.' Pleasantries exchanged, she stalked over and grabbed my ankle, twisting my leg so she could examine my calf. 'Playing with unicorns?' she enquired.

'Something like that,' I said, trying to sound casual. It was reassuring that she could instantly tell what had made the cuts. The talons were relatively distinctive, but even so she must really know her gouges.

She let my ankle drop; her bedside manner required some fine tuning. Then she turned to her black bag and pulled out various Kilner jars filled with noxious-looking substances. She pulled on some disposable gloves, opened one of the jars, scooped out a generous gloop and smeared it on my calf. Interestingly, she didn't just apply the cream directly to the wounded area but seemed to paint a rune of a glyph on my leg. Then she started muttering under her breath.

Her green eyes glowed as she focused on the rune and it started to glow too. As I watched, it shone green and the sticky mixture on my leg gradually disappeared. The wound was still raw and open, and it was still stinging.

Amber snapped off her disposable gloves and pulled on a fresh pair. She selected another jar and the process began anew. She went through ten sets of gloves as she applied potions to my arm and leg and I wanted to complain about her carbon footprint, but that might have sounded ungrateful. Besides, as soon as she discarded each pair they started smouldering. Mrs Dawes picked up the remnants with oven mitts and removed them.

I guess whatever lotions and potions Amber was using on me were pretty dangerous, especially if you didn't know what you were doing. Apparently Amber DeLea knew her stuff. By the time she was packing up her bag, my arm and leg were completely healed. I mean *completely*, not a mark to be seen.

'Thank you,' I said to her gratefully.

She nodded but fixed her eyes on Wilf. 'I'll add it to your account.' She obviously knew he was good for the money.

Wilf nodded. 'Thank you as always, Ms DeLea.' His voice was courteous but cool; it held none of the friendly flirtatious energy that it had when he spoke to me.

'Avoid unicorns,' Amber advised me flatly. She

turned to leave then stilled as she saw Gato. She paused and inclined her head to him, and he bobbed his head in response. Then she gathered her things and left without another word. Super weird.

'She seems nice,' I said into the silence. 'Warm and friendly.'

Archie grinned, 'We don't pay her to be friendly, we pay her to keep us alive.'

'There is that.' I stood up. 'Well, it's been a treat but I've got to fly. Mrs Dawes, I'll drop this nightdress off for you another time.'

'Oh, you keep it, lovely. Floral patterns suit you. But you shouldn't drive. Why don't you stay the night here?' Mrs Dawes looked genuinely distressed at the thought of me behind the wheel.

'Thanks for the offer, but no. My friend will be waiting for me, and I expect she'll be worried by now.' I gave Archie a wave. Despite myself, the little toerag had grown on me. Wilf and Mrs Dawes hugged me, and the housekeeper saw me out.

I motored home to Lucy. She was going to be pissed.

CHAPTER 10

M Y RUINED CLOTHES were on my car seat next to me, as were my handbag and my purse. In the innermost zip compartment of the purse was a baggy full of pink Boost powder. I made a note to store it somewhere safe; if I got stopped, most cops might not look too kindly on it. My PI licence occasionally granted me some latitude with the police, and I might have some success in explaining the Boost was evidence for a case rather than for personal use, but some cops saw my licence and treated me as if I were a criminal. Some didn't like 'amateur' sleuths sticking their nose into what they considered to be police business. My best bet was to avoid any confrontations with the police and drive below the speed limit. And to hide small bags of illegal drugs.

I checked the time and winced. I was pretty late. To soften Lucy's aggravation, I picked up two bottles of our favourite white wine and some Cadbury's Dairy Milk as a peace offering. Yes, I even went into a shop in my nightdress, and yes, I was completely embarrassed, but hopefully it didn't show too much. Gato let out a wheeze, which made me think he was laughing at me too.

It was 9.30 p.m. by the time I parked up at Lucy's. I had a key to her house, but I knocked on the door. Lucy opened the door with a frown, which grudgingly transformed into a smile as she took in the nightdress and the bottles of wine. She giggled and took one of them from me. 'Jinx, what the hell are you wearing?'

I flipped my hair. 'Don't you love it? It's the latest in couture.' I waited a beat. 'Please let me in. I've already been seen in public wearing this.'

Still grinning, she led me into the lounge. 'Explain this.' She gestured at my appearance as she poured us both a big glass of Oyster Bay.

I told her an edited version of a story that had me babysitting a client's son around a farm when he had tripped me over, torn my clothes and got me covered in mud. I explained that he'd insisted on taking me home to clean up, and I'd let him because he had an Audi R8 that I desperately wanted to ride in.

'What about the client's son?' Lucy asked archly. 'Did you want to ride him too?'

'Eww! No. He's like nineteen going on nine. He's a real jerk. Though to be fair, he was pretty nice today.'

Lucy snorted with laughter. 'How could he resist you in that?' She pointed to the lace ruffle around my neck.

I gave her a long look. 'I'll have you know I can make anything look sexy.' I climbed onto her oak coffee table and started doing my best club dancing and hip gyrating. Lucy collapsed onto the floor, helpless with laughter. I turned on some tunes and carried on dancing. Yeah, I could rock this look.

Eventually Lucy's laughter subsided and she joined me on top of the table. We danced, drank and laughed together until 1 a.m., and my soul felt happy.

The next morning my soul did not feel happy, my head did not feel happy and my tummy did not feel happy. I wasn't used to drinking so heavily any more. I showered but decided against going for a run – my insides definitely didn't want to be jiggled about. I dressed and headed downstairs. To my surprise, Lucy was still there beavering away on a laptop.

'Hey,' I greeted her. 'What gives?' It was Friday and she should definitely be in work.

'I called in and said I had an upset tummy and I'd work from home today. I feel rough as hell. Last night was super fun, though. Totally worth it.' She was lying.

'Totally,' I agreed. I was lying too.

I offered to make Lucy's breakfast, which made her go slightly green so I guessed that was a no. I rustled up some food for Gato and made some plain toast for myself. I made a cuppa for Lucy, which she received with a grateful smile. Tea cures most ills, including hangovers.

After breakfast I went upstairs to make a few calls. The first was a quick update to Joyce. I didn't go into too much detail, just that I'd found another murder that I thought was linked to Reggie's and I was investigating it. I wanted to tell her about Reggie's real employment when we were face to face, so I suggested seeing her in the afternoon.

Next I called Amber DeLea and arranged to meet her for lunch at Rosie's. She was brusque and unfriendly, but she agreed. The final call was to Ronan, Reggie's best friend. He said he was free now, and I could pop along to his place of business. He rattled off an address in High Wycombe and I promised to be there in thirty minutes.

'Hey,' I called to Lucy, 'can Gato hang with you? I'll be in and out of the car so it won't be the most thrilling day for him.'

Lucy brightened. 'Sure! We can go for a lunchtime walk together. I'm already feeling a little better and the fresh air will sort me out.'

'Thanks, Luce, I owe you.' I kissed them both and went out the door with my laptop under my arm.

High Wycombe had been one of my stomping grounds with Lucy. As teenagers, we'd hung out at Fast Eddie's and played copious amounts of pool. We'd also hit up the skate parks and drunk alcopops in the park. Good, clean teenage fun. That was back in the days when I'd had lots of friends, before I'd cut them all out. There had been dozens of us dressed in hoodies and ridiculous-ly long jeans, with the occasional dog tags. It had been a fun phase of life. After I'd plastered on dark eye makeup and bright red lipstick, Mum would look at me in my get-up and say, 'You look nice, dear. Have a good time.' Needless to say, that particular phase of my teenage rebellion didn't last long. It was no fun if you didn't get a rise out of your parents.

Driving around High Wycombe made me nostalgic. There was the McDonalds my friend had been mugged in when we were drunk. There was the Boots store where another friend got arrested for shoplifting. There was the tattoo parlour where I got my navel pierced when I was sixteen. Good times.

Ronan's business was on the dingy side of town, situated between a strip joint and a bookmaker's. The only indication it was there was the name: 'Ronan's'. There was a discreet triangle after his name, and that was it. The window was blacked out so I couldn't see what was going on inside.

When I opened the door, I was pleasantly surprised to see a clean, modern office. The floor was wooden laminate and there were two desks with chairs for the workers, and chairs for customers in front of them. Each desk had a computer and a phone. The walls had cute animal motivational posters, like a kitten clinging to a branch with the slogan 'Hang on in there'. I don't know what I'd expected from a piper's business, but it wasn't this. Maybe something similar to a vet's? There were no animals visible, and no receptionist.

Ronan was the sole occupant. He was just-back-from-holiday tanned, with short ginger hair and a strong jawline. He gave me a welcoming smile.

'Jinx,' I introduced myself.

He stood and touched his heart. 'My honour to meet you, Jinx.'

I repeated the greeting and sat down in front of his desk. 'This isn't what I expected for a piper's office,' I commented.

'Piping is a very mobile business. Most pipers have a van and that's about it, but I think having an office adds a more business-like feel that some customers prefer. And, of course, then I can charge more.' *True.* He was grinning at me, charming me with a wink designed to make me feel like a conspirator.

I smiled but let the charm offensive sweep over me. 'What's a piper do day to day?'

He shrugged. 'Depends on the piper. For Common folk, we put out ads like we're animal whisperers, animal behaviourists or animal consultants. They say they're having problems with their dog or horse or whatever, and we ask to work alone with the animal. We communicate with them, work out what the issue is and fix it. For Other folk, we're here for all your magical creature needs – selkies, pixies, unicorns.' He waved a hand expansively. 'Whatever animal you've got a problem with, we'll fix it.'

'How do you communicate with the animals?' I asked out of genuine curiosity.

'For some pipers it's flashes of images, for others they can almost hear the animal's thoughts. Even humans are a lot baser than they try to show. Hearing an animal's thoughts can be ... disturbing sometimes.' *True.*

I could imagine. Hearing a lion's thoughts about how it wanted to eat you would freak me out. Enough about piping. I changed tack. 'And how did you know Reggie?'

Ronan lost the easy smile and looked forlorn. 'We met as kids and we grew up on the same street. We were the only Others around, so we hung out all the time. We went to the same school. He didn't want to be a typical dryad, going into forestry or something. He didn't want his species to define his life choices. I always admired that about him. Reggie was good at maths, so he became an accountant.'

I nodded. 'And when did he tell you he'd gone to work for a drug dealer?'

He blinked then gave me a wry smile. 'Right to it, eh? I knew from the beginning. He didn't want Joyce finding out, and I didn't blame him. I agreed to keep it from her.' *True.*

'Why the drastic change in employment?'

'He was unhappy about it. To be honest, I thought he was being blackmailed.' *True.*

'And you didn't do anything to help him?' I said. My tone was a little accusing. If I thought Lucy was being blackmailed, I'd go to the ends of the earth to stop it.

Ronan tousled his hair with a rough hand and sighed. 'No, I didn't help him. I was involved in some major projects at the time. I figured Reggie was a big boy, he could make his own decisions. He could always have gone to the Connection. Letting himself be blackmailed was a choice.' *True.*

'This *choice* cost him his life,' I said flatly.

'You think the drug dealers had something to do with it?' He raised an eyebrow.

'You don't?' I shot back.

He didn't answer. After a couple of seconds, he cleared his throat. 'I don't know what else I can do to help. I don't know who killed him.' *True.*

'Joyce said you're being really friendly.'

His eyes narrowed and his tone got a little harder. 'What are you insinuating?'

'Nothing,' I said evenly. 'But you've been around a lot.'

'She's my best friend's wife. Of course I'll help her and the kids.' He stood abruptly, all trace of warmth gone. 'I'm sorry but I'll have to see you out. I'm waiting for a call.' *True.*

I nodded and let him usher me through the door. I hadn't made a friend, but I wasn't here to make friends. Despite his annoyance with me, everything he had said to me was one hundred percent true.

CHAPTER 11

I WAS HEADING back to my car when my phone rang, it was an unknown number. I swiped to answer. 'Sharp Security Services,' I said in my best phone voice.

'Jinx?' the voice on the line asked.

'Speaking.'

'It's Emory.'

I stilled. It wasn't a common name. A picture shot into my mind of a mighty red dragon roaring as he clashed with the shield of Mrs H's magic. The flashback was so strong it took me a beat to respond. 'Emory? The dragon?'

There was a pause. 'Yes.'

'You can use a phone with your claws?' I asked curiously.

A longer pause, during which I suspected he was regretting calling me. 'I'm in my human form,' he said finally.

'Sure,' I said breezily, like that had occurred to me. Dragons had a human form? 'So, how can I help?'

'I've heard you're investigating Reggie Evergreen's death.'

'That's right.'

'The Connection thinks his death is related to the sale of a new drug called Boost.'

Elvira was here investigating for the Connection. Steve hadn't seen her files but his own files had been locked and he was told they were above his pay grade. It wouldn't surprise me that Elvira had made the link between Reggie and the dealers. Her access to Steve's files would suggest that she had. I wasn't the woman's biggest fan but she wasn't stupid.

'How do you know that?' I asked. 'I thought dragons weren't part of the Connection.'

'We're not, but I have my sources.'

That didn't surprise me. Stone had told me that Emory was the leader of all of the British dragons so it made sense he would have his own assets, especially if he felt confident rejecting the Connection's resources. 'I'm investigating the drug angle,' I confirmed.

'Good. There's been a spate of drug-related deaths. Overdoses.'

'So I heard.'

'I just got a call that one of mine has died. Yesterday.'

'I'm sorry to hear that.'

'I want to hire you to look into it.'

I wasn't expecting that, but the truth was that my gut was telling me that the drug angle was at the root of Reggie's death. I didn't think it would represent a conflict for me to accept this new case, though I'd have to make sure I didn't look at with blinders on. 'Okay,' I said slowly. 'What information can you give me?'

'I'm heading down shortly. I'll meet you at the victim's residence. Late afternoon, say 4p.m.'

'What's the address?'

'You know it,' he said flatly. 'It's the house in Maidenhead where you stole the vase for Samuel.' He hung up.

Oh shit.

About a year and a half ago, Lord Samuel had hired me to reappropriate a priceless vase. He'd gambled it away in a poker game and wanted me to retrieve it. He'd paid me an exorbitant sum, so off I'd gone with Gato and a bag of sausages to feed to the house owner's pack of attack dogs. It had been a quick job with no real complications, or so I'd thought. If Emory knew about it, then there were complications – I just hadn't known about them. I wondered if *I* was about to become the victim of blackmail.

I blew out a breath and gathered my thoughts. No point worrying about ifs, buts and maybes. I needed to get moving if I was going to keep my appointment with Amber DeLea. I had the impression she was *not* a person to be kept waiting.

I may have sped a little on the way to Rosie's – it happens sometimes – and I made it in the nick of time. Amber was already waiting when I walked in. I gave her a smile, which she didn't return, and asked if she wanted anything. She requested a cappuccino. She looked around me and I couldn't help but think she was checking to see if Gato was with me.

I joined the queue and ordered for us both. The café was quiet and Maxwell was flying solo. 'Hey, Jinx. Chai latte?' he asked.

I grinned. 'You already know my order. You're a superstar. Can I have a sausage sandwich too, and a cappuccino for Miss Frosty over there.' I pointed to Amber.

Maxwell winced and dropped his voice. 'She's the head of the local coven and she's tipped to be the next symposium member when the current witch stands down. Don't piss her off. The last person to do that got shipped off to Alaska.'

I blinked. 'Ten-four. I'll be nice.'

'Super nice,' he advised.

'I'd better get her a muffin too,' I muttered.

Maxwell grinned and gave me a thumbs-up. 'Blueberry is her favourite.' He made her cappuccino in a takeaway cup. When I raised an eyebrow, he explained, 'She won't stay long.'

I paid and carted the food over to the booth where I'd once met Lord Samuel. I passed Amber her cappuccino and muffin. She didn't thank me. All righty.

'Thanks for agreeing to meet with me,' I started.

'Hopefully I won't need to take up too much of your time.'

'Take as much as you want,' she said, sipping her drink. 'I'll be invoicing for it.'

I didn't take offence; I ran my own business and I charged for my services too. 'Fair enough. What's your rate?'

She quoted an hourly rate which made me wince internally, but I agreed to it without flinching. Since this was business rather than a favour, I got straight to it. 'I'm assuming you're not squeamish. Can I show you some photos of dead bodies?'

She raised one perfectly manicured eyebrow but nodded.

I reached into my handbag and pulled out the three files. The first was Miller's. I passed it to her, and she opened the cover. At the front was the photograph of the scene of his death. I didn't really think she'd have anything to add, but it was best to check. 'Does anything strike you as unusual here?' I asked.

She pored over the picture. 'Well, for starters,' she said, 'this is a car accident scene. But *this*,' she pointed to the metal projectile in his chest, 'is a tree. Well, a branch to be exact.' She murmured some words and her eyes flashed.

I blinked. 'Excuse me? I could have sworn it was metal.' I looked at the picture again; now it was quite clearly a tree branch, a straight piece of wood – it even had bark on it. How had I ever thought it was metal?

'It was enchanted,' she confirmed darkly. 'A witch enchanted the wood to make it look like it was metal, possibly at the scene. It would appear to be metal both on examination and in any visual representation. The latter is a tricky piece of magic.' She frowned and checked the address of the scene. 'Local,' she muttered to herself, her frown deepening.

She got out her phone and took a few photos. I didn't object; Miller wasn't my client, and Maxwell had said not to piss her off.

She set the photo aside and looked at me expectantly. I put away Miller's file and pulled out Reggie's. She flicked through the gory pictures. 'Griffin,' she said, passing them back to me.

It was my turn to raise an eyebrow. 'Are you sure?' I asked.

She gave me an icy glare. 'Yes.' *True.*

I packed away Reggie's file and passed her the one for my parents. She took it and flicked through it, pausing at the first picture. 'Ah,' she said slowly. 'You're the Sharps' daughter. I knew there was something familiar about you – and, of course, there was their hell hound, Isaac. I should have realised.'

'You knew my parents?' I said it with some surprise. She didn't look much older than me, perhaps in her early thirties.

She nodded, easily reading the confusion on my face. 'I'm older than I look.'

'What can you tell me about them?' I asked eagerly.

'Nothing that you want to hear,' she responded slowly. *True.* She turned back to the crime-scene photos. 'Griffin,' she said again with certainty.

Everything in me stilled. I *knew* it wasn't a home invasion. 'Do you know why my parents left the Other realm?' I tried to keep the hope out of my voice.

'Presumably to avoid this.' She tapped the photo. *Lie.* She stood and picked up her bag. 'No charge, and I owe you one boon since you brought the Miller issue to my attention. Good day, Miss Sharp.' She grabbed her cappuccino and muffin and left.

I ate my sausage sandwich. The meeting had been helpful on lots of levels. I knew I should be more focused on Reggie, but I was conflicted by the need to find out about my parents. A huge part of me was relieved to find out that their deaths *had* been Other, not a home invasion gone wrong. I felt vindicated. For all these years I hadn't found a trace of their killer, but I'd been looking in the wrong realm. And Amber knew why my parents had left the Other. I didn't get a chance to dig into it today but I would – and soon.

I took my empty plate and cup up to the counter. 'She said she wouldn't charge me,' I commented to Maxwell. 'How come?'

'Did you help her?'

'She seemed to think so. She was suggesting a witch was involved in covering up a local crime scene.'

He nodded. 'That'd do it. As head of the coven, all witches answer to her. All work is vetted and allocated though her. If someone has done a job without her knowledge, then she has a rogue witch. If the Connection found out, it would put her back years politically. If she can't control her own coven, how can she seek to control all witches as the symposium member?'

'Huh. Politics in the Other seem a little harsh.'

'They need to be because all of us are dangerous. Take me and Roscoe: if we went rogue, we could burn down half of London before we were stopped. It would threaten the Verdict and threaten the Common's ideas about the Other. Our symposium member is a fire elemental called Benedict. Believe me, if you put a toe out of line he'll visit you and make sure you regret it. Each member of the symposium must be seen as strong. If we lose that, we'll have chaos.' He dropped his voice low when he spoke about Benedict and his fear was palpable.

'You're scared of your leader?'

'Shitless,' Maxwell declared. 'Before Roscoe rode to your rescue a few weeks ago, he had to get it cleared by Benedict. Benedict lives to make Roscoe's life difficult because he hates same-sex couples – apparently we're failing our species by not procreating. Roscoe only got clearance to help you because you'd been introduced in his hall, and even Benedict couldn't ignore that obligation.'

I blinked. 'Hall?' I asked.

'It's what we call portal locations,' Maxwell explained. 'Roscoe is the guardian of this hall. I'm just the back up.'

'Does it bother you to pose as a café worker just to look after the portal?'

Maxwell grinned. 'Oh no. The portal was here first and Roscoe was allocated to be its guardian. He chose to make it a café as our cover and we love it. We import all of the cakes and sandwiches rather than making them ourselves, but we love making coffee and chatting with people. It's a great way to get intel.'

He was right: I'd just told him all about Amber having a rogue witch. Oops. Thankfully, I hadn't told him anything about Emory. I'd have to be careful what I said when I was in here in the future. But at least Maxwell had given me the heads up. And it had made me remember that just because I liked someone, it didn't mean that they were trustworthy. Like Stone.

I gave Maxwell a finger wave and headed out. It was too early to drive to Maidenhead, but I'd make a few calls.

First I called Mo to check on his progress. He confirmed that Reggie's laptop was next on his list; he'd get it to me by tomorrow. The delay chafed but it couldn't be helped. Next I tugged out my own laptop and sent emails to a few clients, noting down the time I spent so I could invoice for it.

I gave Hes a call and was relieved when she sounded upbeat and cheerful. We discussed a couple of accounts that she was going to bill for me, then she told me she'd had a call from a Mr Emory and she'd given him my mobile number. I commented dryly that a heads up would have been nice – perhaps then I wouldn't have made the idiotic comment about dragon claws and phones.

With Emory fresh in my mind, I plugged in the Maidenhead address and set off. I tried to tell myself that the curling in my gut wasn't caused by excitement. Yeah, right.

CHAPTER 12

WE WERE IN the depths of winter, only a few weeks away from Christmas, so meeting Emory at 4p.m. meant that the sun was just dipping below the horizon. Last time I'd been here it had been at 9p.m. on the summer solstice, and the sun had been in much the same position.

This time, however, I drove up the gravel pathway rather than approaching by boat. The white, castellated house looked much the same, except now it was a hive of activity. A number of large vans were being loaded up. As I drew up, I saw several bubble-wrapped portraits being carried onto them, followed by a chaise longue. The dragon had barely been dead a day and the vultures had already descended. I tried not to be too judgemental but a part of me was shocked; Conrad's body was barely cold.

As I climbed out and beeped my car locked, I looked around for the vicious attack dogs that I remembered from my last visit. Instead, I saw three unicorns corralled on the front lawn. I frowned. That didn't make any sense. I had first-hand experience of how vicious they could be;

if they'd been here when I last visited, how had I got past them? Maybe the dragon had upgraded his security following my visit – it had been pretty lax.

The double wooden doors into the house were flung open. I hadn't used the front door last time I was here, I'd slunk in the back way like a thief in the night because – well, I *was* a thief in the night. This time I used the front door.

As I walked in, I surveyed the scene. There were probably ten removal men, all dressed from head to toe in black. They looked more like thieves than I did. They were carting objects away from each room, some packed in boxes, some bubble wrapped. Everything was being taken.

At the bottom of the wide staircase a man was directing the operation. He was tall, broad and muscular. His black hair had a side parting and his dark eyebrows framed emerald-green eyes. A five o'clock shadow whiskered his chiselled chin. There were no triangles adorning his forehead. He wasn't in dragon form, but I recognised the unforgettable eyes: it was Emory. He was dressed in corporate smart, and his black shirt and suit looked like they'd cost more than my car. My suit trousers and white shirt were off the rack but I refused to feel self-conscious about it.

'Jinx,' he greeted me. It was hard to reconcile the man before me with the eighteen-foot-tall ruby-red dragon I'd seen before. Gone were the spikes and the teeth that could rip you in half. I had to work at reminding myself that he was far more than just the handsome man before me.

'Emory,' I responded. He hadn't done the whole 'my honour to meet you' routine, so I cut it too. Technically we'd met a few times before, albeit in passing. And, of course, there was the time we'd worked together to get to Mrs H before she murdered Nate and Hes. Good times.

'Follow me,' he ordered brusquely. Despite his tone, I followed; well, he was the client.

He led me upstairs into one of the rooms. I was sure it would be Bedroom Seven. Bingo. Behind the ordinary-looking door was a huge floor-to-ceiling vault. It was open and more men were removing the contents. One of them was sitting at the security console. He was a huge hulking man, all muscle and bulk, and I wouldn't have wanted to meet him in a dark alley. He was ginger; I wondered if playground bullying had contributed to his desire to develop a stacked physique.

'Tom, leave us,' Emory directed.

'Yes, Prime,' the man at the desk responded. He gave a sharp whistle and the others followed him out.

The security console had a number of screens, each showing four camera angles. There were a lot of cameras. Huh: I hadn't spotted *any* cameras when I was here last time.

Emory read my thoughts. 'The cameras are enchanted so they're not usually seen,' he explained. He pulled out a DVD labelled *Incident 2019*. I winced. I knew what I was going to see next.

He put the disk into a slot on the computer hard drive and pressed play. He moved the footage forward and clicked on one of the camera angles; he was clearly familiar with the footage. The screen showed the lawn outside. The images were grainy, but I could clearly see Gato stalking forward in full Battle Cat mode. He had a bunch of sausages in his mouth, which he laid down at the unicorns' clawed feet.

As the unicorns turned their backs towards me, I raced across the lawn to the kitchen door. What on earth? I vividly remembered a pack of vicious dogs, not unicorns. I guessed that my mind, then still in the Common, had substituted something that made sense.

Emory clicked onto another camera angle and I watched as I entered the kitchen and carefully closed the door. I leaned against it, closed my eyes in relief and then... I disappeared.

'What?' I exclaimed involuntarily, moving forwards to examine the screen. I frowned and turned to Emory, 'Someone's tampered with the disc,' I accused.

He looked at me with interest. 'No, they haven't.' He fast-forwarded the footage and took us to another room. A vase lifted off the table it was standing on and then winked out of existence. He changed camera angles again and I watched, gaping with shock, as a figurine tumbled off a table of its own volition before it was swept under a side table.

'Huh,' I said intelligently. I blinked several times.

'You're invisible,' Emory explained.

'It does look that way,' I agreed reluctantly. 'But how?'

He shrugged. 'With the IR, I imagine.'

I shook my head. 'I was only introduced about eight weeks ago. This was nearly two years ago.'

Emory dragged the footage back to the opening sequence and paused it as I leaned against the inside of the kitchen door. He dragged the mouse up to the triangle in the middle of my forehead. 'And how do you explain that, Miss Sharp?'

I sat down. There it was, in black and white. I'd been in the Other before I'd been introduced, and I had no memory of it. Someone had cleared my mind.

Suddenly I remembered Wilf's odd appearance at my house that night, and something clicked into place. I hauled out my phone and rang him.

'Jinx!' he greeted me happily. 'How is the calf?'

'You cleared my mind!' I snapped accusingly.

There was a beat of silence. 'Not me,' Wilf said softly. 'You called me after the Maidenhead job, Gato had portalled you to protect you, as I'd hoped he would.'

'That's why you insisted I take Gato?'

'Yes. I knew Gato was a hell hound and I suspected he'd bonded with you. That could only happen if you were Other. Despite all the indications, you didn't seem to have been introduced, and you were oblivious to our realm. I set about trying to get you into the Other realm, but only a Connection inspector or detective could introduce you and I didn't have one to hand. You could also be introduced if your life was in danger. So, I needed to put you in danger. I lost the vase to Conrad and sent you on a retrieval job.'

'You sent me into a dragon's den on purpose! With unicorns!'

'And Gato!' he protested. 'Gato wouldn't have let harm come to you.'

'Later on, with Hester, you threw me together with Stone.'

'Well, yes. Danger didn't work, but I hoped Stone would introduce you. As he did.' Wilf was a little smug about that.

I didn't know whether to thank him or punch him. 'Jesus, Wilf,' I muttered finally.

'Still friends?' he enquired lightly.

That made me laugh. 'Still friends,' I agreed. And for the first time, it was true. Wilf had been looking out for me for years. In my mind, and my heart, he had finally made the shift from friendly acquaintance to my pack, a small but elite group. He'd be delighted he'd made the cut, but I wouldn't be telling him any time soon.

I sighed. 'If it wasn't you who cleared my mind, who was it?'

'I can't help you with that. You said an old man stopped by your flat for sugar but you didn't know him. I'd say it was him, but I've never managed to track him down.'

'Okay. Thanks, Wilf.'

'Amber can break the clearance for you, if you want.'

I did want; I hated the idea that someone had played God with my mind. That Stone had compelled me was bad enough; to imagine someone taking away my memories outraged me still further. I was going to find out who'd done this to me and why. And then I'd make them sorry as hell for interfering in my life.

For a moment I felt like a terrible hypocrite because I'd done the same to Dave, but I'd only cleared his mind of a couple of minutes and it was a matter of life and death. Whoever had done this to me had better have as good an explanation.

'Yes,' I said tightly. 'I want it broken. I'll call her.'

'I can arrange it for you,' Wilf offered.

'No, it's okay. She owes me a favour.'

'Does she now?' Wilf said, intrigued. 'And how did you manage that between yesterday and today?'

'None of your business.' I paused. 'Thanks, Wilf.' I hung up.

Emory had been listening. 'You've no idea who cleared you?' he asked. I shook my head. 'Interesting,' he mused.

I frowned as I remembered that there had been a photo on the wall in this house that had felt important. 'Can I see any framed pictures that were in the hall?'

Emory raised an elegant eyebrow, pulled out his phone and dialled a number. 'Leave Van 2 on the drive for a moment. We need to check the hall contents.' He hung up. Some people have no phone manners. 'We'll get to that in a minute. For now, look at this.'

He ejected the DVD and inserted another one. This showed someone outside, approaching the door. He was hooded, but I recognised him straight away because he was fresh in my mind. It was Dave, Archie's friendly dealer.

'That's Dave,' I told Emory. 'He's a drug dealer, a small fish – he barely knows what pond he's swimming in. Hell, he barely knows the day of the week.'

Emory gave me an approving glance; I was already adding value to his investigation. I straightened under his gaze. 'Okay,' he said. 'We'll hit up Dave later. Can you arrange that?'

I nodded and texted Archie, asking him to arrange for me to meet Dave again. This time I would go alone. I warned Archie that this meeting might burn bridges, but I got an immediate response saying that he'd let me know once a time was set. Maybe he wasn't such a little shit after all.

Emory stood up. 'Let's check the van.'

We went out onto the drive and I followed him to Van 2. He opened the back and gestured for me to go inside. I climbed in and started looking through a box of framed pictures. It was difficult because the images were distorted by the bubble wrap, but I came to one and my gut sang. Bingo.

I unwrapped it carefully. It was a photograph of my parents next to a giant red dragon. A man was sitting astride the dragon. My heart thundering, I turned to show it to Emory.

I squeaked as I found him already next to me. 'Jesus, make some noise next time, Ninja dragon,' I muttered.

He looked faintly amused. He glanced at the picture and back to me. 'Family?' he asked. 'There's a resemblance.'

I nodded. 'My parents. Is this the dragon that's died?'

Emory shook his head. 'No, this is someone else.'

'Can you arrange for me to meet this dragon?' I asked desperately.

'Perhaps.' Emory's tone was non-committal. 'Come, let's go and see the body. You can keep the photo.'

I stashed the photo and its frame in my car. Emory might think this conversation was done but it wasn't. One way or another, I was going to find this dragon and the man next to it. The Other realm has been involved in my parents' deaths and the Other realm would help me solve it.

For now, I focused on the matter at hand. I followed Emory as he led me back into the mansion. 'The body hasn't been removed?'

Emory shook his head. 'No. As I'm sure you surmised last time you were here, Conrad was a younger dragon, still very much in his acquiring phase. Over the years we've found that if we don't remove the hoard before we report a death, the wealth gets "secured" by the Connection. It's held as evidence and it takes a long time to petition for its release. Once it *is* released, there have been frequent allegations of items going missing. Now we do it this way – we clear the house and then notify the Connection.'

That made sense and painted the household removal in a somewhat different light. 'It's awful you have to do that,' I commented.

'Humans only have so much self-control. They can't look at all that wealth and not slip the odd diamond into their pocket.'

'That's a cynical point of view.'

'Realistic,' he countered.

I couldn't really argue with that; besides, I wasn't sure he was wrong. Personally, in the face of all that wealth I'd only grabbed the vase and run. I hadn't been tempted by all the jewels. I'd been hired for one job and one job alone, and that's what I carried out. I might technically be a thief, but that made me feel like I still had a loose hold on my morals.

'I got the impression that dragons were rare,' I said. 'I didn't think there were enough of you to have frequent deaths to deal with.'

'We are few on a human scale. We may be largely immortal in nature, but we can still be killed.'

I blinked. Dragons were *immortal*? I tried to act like this wasn't new information. 'Sure, but the Connection has been in place what – eighty years? How many deaths have you had?'

'Four,' Emory confirmed.

'Across the UK?'

'Across Europe.'

'Huh.'

Emory didn't comment on my eloquence, he just opened the door. The room behind it was huge and cloaked in darkness. All the curtains were drawn. Perhaps in times gone by this massive room would have been a ballroom, but now it held a dragon.

For a moment, I thought Conrad was sleeping but his blue-and-silver scales were dull and his chest wasn't moving. It wasn't a gruesome scene, but I sensed a deep sadness emitting from Emory. 'You knew him?' I asked gently.

'Of course. I'm the Prime.'

'Uh-huh. And that means…?'

'I'm the leader of the dragons here,' he said. *True.*

'In the UK?'

'Yes.'

The moon was up and full, which would light the room without us flicking on the overhead lights. I stepped towards a window and went to draw back a curtain but Emory caught my hand. 'Don't. He must be kept in darkness until his final light.'

I looked around dubiously. Even if there was a clue, I wasn't going to see it in this gloom.

'Here.' Emory let out a breath that coalesced into a ball of flickering flames. He directed it to float near me. 'Flame light is allowed.'

I glared at the ball of flames. How was that possible? Emory wasn't even in the Other. 'But you haven't got a triangle!' I objected. Every single time I thought I'd got a handle on the rules of the realm, something broke them.

'I'm a magical creature. Like the unicorns and pixies, we're not marked.'

I rolled my eyes. 'You're as human as I am.'

'No,' he said firmly. 'I'm not. I'm a dragon that can shift into human form, not a human who can shift into dragon form.'

'You accept your classification as a creature?' I asked with some surprise.

'No.' His voice was hard. 'I do not.'

Oops. I'd stumbled upon something there. I turned my attention away from Emory back to poor old Conrad and used the floating light to examine him. I wasn't sure what I could bring to the party because I didn't know what a live dragon *should* look like, let alone a dead one.

Finally I made my way around his body to his head. Conrad's eyes were wide open and it seemed wrong to see them vacant. I reached over to close his eyelids, glancing to Emory to check he had no objections. He watched me coolly but didn't say anything. If I hadn't felt the grief pouring off him, I'd have thought he was unaffected by Conrad's death.

As I touched Conrad's eyelids, I was hit by a rush of joy and happiness that took my breath away. I closed my eyes against it and I was transported.

Conrad was flying, soaring, laughing for the joy of it. He let out a bugle call and flew downwards, getting a ground rush before leaping up at the last minute. He'd taken Boost and he was soaring high, higher than ever before. He trumpeted to the moon and flew up, up to the stars. He could reach the moon. His mama would be so proud if he could reach the moon like Erasmus had done. His lungs were straining and burning, but he knew he could do it. He flew towards the moon until he flew no more.

I came back to myself. I was on the floor next to Conrad, crying helplessly. He had been so young, so joyful, so full of happiness. He hadn't even realised he was dying.

I wasn't even crying for him. I was crying for his mama, whom he had loved so much, who would be broken by losing him. I knew grief like it was my own shadow, and I hated it when it struck someone else.

I took a few deep breaths and wiped away my tears. 'He was hallucinating,' I said finally when I could speak without sobbing. 'Dreaming of flying to the moon. He was happy. He had no idea he was dying. There was no pain, no sadness. He was joyous.'

'You're an empath,' Emory said accusingly.

I nodded. 'Yes.' I stood up shakily. 'It's not widely known, so I'd be grateful if you'd keep it to yourself.'

Emory gave a slight nod, but I didn't doubt it was as binding as Volderiss's gory blood oath. 'Who is Erasmus?' I asked.

Emory stilled. In that moment, I knew he truly believed I'd seen Conrad's last moments. 'A legend.'

'Conrad was thinking of his mama. How proud she'd be...'

Emory's grief sharpened but his face remained unaffected. 'I'll make sure she knows.'

I was never going to play poker with him. I didn't prod him further. We all had our masks. I needed to regain mine.

CHAPTER 13

A FTER MY EMOTIONAL breakdown, I felt I needed to regain some of my street cred. Luckily Archie came through. I had a meeting with Dave by the lake at Black Park at 8p.m. The car park would be closed and various gates would be locked, but Archie assured me I'd get in easily enough.

It was 6 p.m. now and most of Conrad's treasures had been hauled away, leaving behind a shell of a house and a cold body. Emory called the Connection and reported the death. As we waited for them and/or the crossover police to arrive, Emory dismissed most of his men. We waited in the now-vacant lounge. Emory breathed a ball of fire into the fireplace and we sat side by side on the one remaining sofa. It would have been cosy if there hadn't been a dead body in the next room.

'Are all the men dressed in black dragons?' I asked curiously.

Emory shook his head. 'Dragon brethren.'

I waited to see if he would elaborate but he didn't. 'So dragon brethren are...?'

Emory cast me an amused look but didn't respond.

'Are they like groupies or…?'

Emory almost smiled. 'Like brethren.'

'That's a pretty old word.'

'We're an old people.'

I nodded. 'Sure, what with the immortality and all. So you're the king?'

'Prime.'

'Right. Prime. How old are you?' I asked.

'How old are you?' he countered.

'Twenty-five. See? It's an easy question. How old are you?' I repeated.

'It's a rude question,' he said finally, though he looked amused rather than offended.

I examined him. 'You don't look old.'

His lips twitched. 'I am.'

'Like a hundred? Or a thousand?'

Emory shrugged. 'Something like that.'

'Which?'

He smiled.

I sighed. 'Has anyone ever told you that you're infuriating?'

'A few.' He was still smiling.

I rolled my eyes but inwardly I was pleased. Emory's feeling of grief had lessened as he'd been distracted by my antics.

Someone pounded on the front door and we both

rose to investigate. Emory cast me a sidelong glance, but he didn't stop me going with him. It was Steve, in full uniform, with his squad car parked up behind him. 'Hi, Steve!' I gave him a friendly smile.

'Jinx! Of course you're here.' His welcoming grin faded and his eyes widened as he took in Emory standing next to me. 'Prime.' He greeted Emory in a strangled voice and gave a deep bow.

'Was I supposed to do that?' I asked Emory.

A smile flashed across his face; it was there and gone in a moment. 'I'll forgive you.'

'Thanks. I'll work on my courtesy for next time.'

Emory focused on Steve. 'Detective…?'

'Marley, sir.'

'Come this way.' He led us back to Conrad's body. Everything about Emory said he was a man used to being obeyed. He delivered commands like he breathed: effortlessly and without thought. I wondered how long he had been Prime. Heck, I wondered how long he had *been*.

'Are you the only Other detective that works here?' I asked Steve. 'Every time I call, I get you.'

'There aren't that many crossovers in these parts – the Other population isn't very big here. I tend to catch it whether it's my shift or not.' He gave me a sidelong glance. 'It would help if you didn't incite violence.'

'Me? Incite violence? I don't know what you're talking about.' I protested. *Lie.*

'The Sandersons?' He was referring to one of my earlier PI snafus. I'd emailed photos of the cheating to one of the spouses when said cheating had still been occurring. How was I to know the cuckolded spouse would instantly recognise the location and come and smackdown the cheater? Live and learn.

'That was years ago! I've come a long way since then. Now I make sure the cheater is done before I do the reveal. By the way, did you ever find out what happened with them?' I asked nosily.

'Divorce. A colleague was called to their house when she was throwing his clothes off their property.'

'Ah. Well, good for her.'

'Indeed.'

We arrived at the big room and fell silent. Chatter wasn't appropriate here. There were two brethren in the room keeping watch over the body, ensuring it was not touched by moonlight. Emory breathed another small fireball and directed it to flow over Steve. Steve took out his camera and started taking photographs.

A bell thundered through the house. I guess the doorbell had to be pretty loud when the house was this gargantuan. I started towards the front door with Emory following. He gestured for me to open it then he hung back in the shadows. I guess he was willing for me to take point, though I wasn't sure why.

It was Inspector Elvira Garcia. She was dressed in her

Connection uniform of a black suit and white shirt which looked painted on. She was also wearing ridiculously high heels. Her dark hair was tumbling down her shoulders and her lips were maroon red against her bronzed skin. She had three triangles on her forehead. She was stunning. Frankly, I looked like a troll standing next to her.

I gave her a friendly wave. 'Hey, Elvira.'

'Jinx,' Elvira snarled. 'I thought it was your voice the other day, but I dismissed it because you're supposed to be in Liverpool. It *was* you. What in hell were you thinking of, releasing unicorns?'

'I don't know what you're talking about,' I said, eyes wide. *Lie.*

Elvira rolled her dark eyes. 'Sure. If that's what you're going with. Where's Stone?'

I blinked. 'I have no idea,' I said honestly. 'I haven't seen him since the battle.'

That seemed to cheer her up. 'Good. So, what are you doing here? Did you find more unicorns to release?' Her tone was laden with derision.

'There are three,' I acknowledged, 'but these ones have been secured.'

'Glad to see the last experience taught you something,' she muttered.

'Unicorns are freaking scary,' I admitted.

That made her laugh despite herself. 'You're telling

me. It took fifteen of us to round them up one at a time. You'll be happy to know they were sent to a safe pasture.'

I gave her a vague smile, not conceding anything.

'Why are you here?' she asked.

'I've been hired to investigate the death.'

Elvira glared at me. 'What fool hired you?' she sneered.

'This one,' Emory said mildly, stepping out of the shadows.

Elvira's eyes widened. 'Prime!' She bowed, not as low as Steve had but a bow nonetheless. I decided that Emory liked making an entrance and secretly observing people. Emory was sneaky. I liked him already.

'This way,' Emory said. He lengthened his stride so Elvira could hardly keep up. Heh-heh-heh. 'No light,' he cautioned.

Elvira opened her mouth to say something smart but closed it with a clack. Best not to sass the prime dragon, even if he wasn't part of the almighty Connection.

Emory nodded to the two brethren, his orders implicit, then he turned to me. 'We'd better leave for our next appointment.'

'You're coming with me?' I asked, surprised.

'Yes.'

I wanted to argue with him but not in front of Elvira, so I nodded and he followed me out. He climbed into the passenger side of my Ford Focus. I wish I'd hoovered it recently, but then I hadn't known I was going to have dragon royalty in my car.

I plotted a course for Black Park. 'Listen,' I started. 'I'm not sure you coming with me to meet Dave is a good idea. He might not talk as much, and he'll definitely freak out if he knows who you are.'

'I *want* him to know who I am. I want his boss to know who I am. Let them know I'm after them. Scared people make mistakes.'

'You're a little scary. You know that, right?'

He grinned wickedly. 'I'm a lot scary.'

'A little,' I countered. His smile widened and he didn't argue. 'Okay, fine. You can come – but let me do the talking first.'

'I have no issue with that.' He switched on the radio and tuned it to a classical station.

'Do you like classical music because you were alive when Mozart was composing?' I asked.

He laughed. 'I like classical music because it's beautiful. Things of beauty should be admired.' He gave me a long look full of meaning. I missed whatever the meaning was; he couldn't have been referring to little old ragtag me.

'Anyway,' I smoothly changed the topic, 'talk to me about drugs.'

He blinked. 'Well, you know about the classification system?' Everyone is a comedian.

'Drugs and dragons,' I clarified.

'Normally, we can drink alcohol until the cows come home. We can take drugs until more cows come home. Neither affects us a whit.'

'But Boost does?'

'So it appears,' Emory said grimly. 'Our younger dragons are impetuous and eager to experience something long denied them.'

'Have you sent out a text to everyone: "do not take; deadly"?'

'A text?' He grinned. 'Dragons are an old-fashioned people.'

'Right. And they have brethren. No texting.'

'I've sent a mailshot,' he admitted.

That made me snigger. 'Really? Not even emails?'

He shook his head balefully. 'Most don't even have computers.'

Now that he mentioned it, Conrad hadn't had any technology save for the lighting and the vault security room. 'You've got to roll with the times,' I counselled.

'Try telling that to a wing of dragons.'

'A wing?'

'Our collective term.'

'I figured you guys for a clutch of dragons.'

'That sounds like a group of birds.'

'When the wing fits…'

Emory glared at me. I gave him a wink but fell silent. Sometimes discretion is the better part of valour.

CHAPTER 14

WE PARKED UP much closer to the lake than I had with Archie. Firstly, I didn't know the woods like the back of my hand, and secondly, we were running close to time. It was 7.50 p.m. The clock was ticking.

I grabbed a torch from the back of my car and slung on my somewhat damaged leather jacket. It was cold enough for me to pull on my hat, too. Emory was still in a suit. 'Are you warm enough?' I enquired.

I saw a flash of teeth in the dark. 'Yes, Mum.'

I stuck my tongue out in response. Okay, so he was my client, but for some reason he was drawing out the silliness in me. And besides, he hadn't signed a contract. At the moment I was being hired by Joyce, not the dragon prime.

I switched on the torch, and we headed down to the lakeside. I expect Emory could have provided us with some floating orbs of light to illuminate our way but that didn't seem particularly discreet.

Dave was by the lake. Today his dreadlocks were spilling out of a blue bobble hat. He glanced towards me but his eyes didn't light up with recognition. The mind clearance was still in place. Cigarette butts were littered at his feet; Dave had obviously been here for some time and Dave was nervous.

'It's a set up,' I breathed to Emory as I peered into the shadows.

Suddenly movement burst towards us, unnaturally fast and unnaturally attractive. Vampyrs.

Across the oceans between us, I felt Nate's awareness of my alarm. Poor Nate – this was the second panic attack in as many days. I barely had time to think, let alone reassure him, because I needed to focus. I didn't have Gato so I had no access to the Third realm. I didn't have any weapons, bar a small knife in my boot. As I went to reach for it, my hand detoured of its own volition to my jacket pocket. Glimmer. It shouldn't be there, but I was grateful that it was.

I wasted no time in drawing and unwrapping it. The last scraps of Mrs H's lilac skirt fell to the ground just as a vampyr was upon me. Glimmer sang and I felt its fierce joy at being used, being useful. It shot out and sliced the vampyr's throat with a speed that I couldn't comprehend. The dagger barely felt any resistance as it bit into his neck. Thick blood sprayed across me but I didn't have time to be revolted because now there was movement behind me.

I spun on my heel and a second vampyr encountered

Glimmer with deadly consequences – though I guess technically vampyrs are already dead. These two were now extra dead. The one standing before me took a moment to realise he'd died again. He blinked twice and looked down at the blood pouring down his body, then he fell to his knees. He raised his hands to his neck and toppled over.

I would probably freak out later but, for now, I needed to stay alive.

I looked around. Dave was running off into the distance, so I guessed he wasn't fond of a fight. There were three more vampyrs – but I was the least of their concerns.

Emory had transformed. His ruby-red scales were glittering in the moonlight and his claws were dripping with blood. He reared back onto his hind legs and roared his fury into the night as he sliced and diced the vampyrs.

The vampyrs had probably thought five of them against little old me was more than sufficient, and they would probably have been right, but I wasn't alone. The prime dragon seemed a little annoyed with them. He toyed with them, slashing and scraping, using his tail to haul them back to the fight when they tried to escape. Emory must have been eighteen feet long, longer if you counted his tail, yet his hulking size didn't inhibit him in the slightest. He was *fast*, almost faster than the vampyrs.

One enterprising vampyr got close enough to try to

bite him but his fangs slid harmlessly off the dragon's scales. In response, he was picked up and thrown against a tree where he slid silently to the floor. The vampyrs seemed wholly unprepared to fight a dragon; they had no weapons and, frankly, they had no skills. The remaining two vampyrs took advantage of Emory's focus on their comrade and ran away. Emory watched them coolly and I saw him decide to let them go.

I wiped Glimmer on the remnants of Mrs H's skirt. It was happy to have been used, full of *Otherness*. 'Behave,' I muttered, and I put it back in my jacket pocket. It stopped singing and settled down.

Emory's green eyes turned to me. If I'd had to place the emotion in them I would have said concern, but I felt strangely unafraid in the face of a gigantic dragon. After all, my parents had been friends with a dragon too. I wanted to stroke him, to feel the texture of those scales. Were they rough or smooth? I resisted the urge; I suspected stroking your potential boss was frowned on.

'Hey,' I said. 'Care to switch back to human so you're a little more discreet?'

Emory shimmered and there he was in human form once again, complete with sharp suit and five o'clock shadow.

'Huh,' I muttered, thinking of the werewolves' transformation. 'How come you get to keep your clothes when you change?'

Emory flashed me a grin. 'Disappointed?' he asked.

'No,' I replied, a shade too emphatically. *Lie*. Dammit. I tried to keep the blush off my cheeks and cleared my throat. 'Anyway, let's go and see if that vampyr you threw against the tree is still alive.'

The two I had sliced had disappeared into dust. I told myself firmly that this was because they had lived full and good lives and they vanished because they were just so *old*. I wasn't evil for killing them. Anyway, they were trying to kill me, which wasn't very friendly. I wasn't sure that rationale would stop the nightmares.

The vampyr that Emory had chucked at the tree was still out cold. I gave him a little tap on his cheek. He didn't respond but he hadn't disappeared into dust either, so he was still alive. Or, more accurately, undead.

'He's out cold. How do we get information from him?' I asked.

'Use the IR,' Emory suggested.

I blinked. I'd been a part of this crazy realm for two months, but I still kept forgetting I could use the IR. I gathered my intention. I wanted the vampyr to wake up, I needed him to wake up. 'Wake up,' I ordered.

His eyes snapped open, and he surged forward towards me. Emory pinned him back against the tree.

'Hello.' I greeted the vampyr with a finger wave. 'I'm the one you were going to kill. Who gave you orders to be here?' I was certain that I was the target, not Emory. The vampyrs had been ill-prepared to fight a dragon.

While I watched, he shifted and got visibly younger. He now looked like he was sixteen at best, and I had to remind myself that he must be far older. Slumped unconscious, he'd looked at least my age. He was using vampyr tricks to make me feel sympathetic, to downgrade his threat level.

'Nice try,' I commented, 'but we both know you're not an innocent kid. The dragon here will have no compunction in punching the snot out of you.' I didn't know that for certain, but it seemed likely. Emory had attacked the vampyrs forcefully and he hadn't held back. It didn't bother him if they survived or re-died.

To prove my point Emory smashed his fist into the vampyr's face a few times. I held him back on the third punch. 'You need to give him the opportunity to talk,' I pointed out.

His eyes glittered dangerously. 'Do I?'

'For Conrad, yes.' That did it. The anger banked, not gone but controlled. Emory nodded curtly and once again switched to holding the vampyr against the tree.

'Which clan are you?' I asked conversationally.

The boy vampyr glared at me and said nothing. I sighed; okay, it wasn't my favourite thing to do but I was going to have to compel him or we'd get nowhere. 'Which clan are you?' I asked again. This time I put some power behind it.

The boy's eyes went glassy. 'Clan Wokeshire.'

'And who gave you the order to come here tonight?'

He tried to resist the question, so I pressed a little harder. 'Lord Wokeshire,' he spat.

Interesting. Maybe the head of the clan was part of the drug ring, maybe he just liked Boost, or maybe he just didn't like me. I struck the latter off my mental list right away. Who wouldn't like me?

'Were your orders to kill me?'

'Yes.' *True.*

'Do you know Reggie Greengrass, Conrad the dragon, or Freddie Miller?'

He frowned at me. 'No.' *True.*

'Have you seen any vampyrs taking Boost?'

The boy really tried to resist that one. 'Yes,' he finally admitted. 'Lord Wokeshire's daughter. Mererid Wokeshire.'

Maybe Lord Wokeshire was protecting his daughter. Maybe she was the one hip-deep with the drug cartel. Either way, it looked like we were going to see some more of their brethren.

'Do you have any questions?' I asked Emory. He shook his head. 'Let him go then.'

Emory's jaw clenched. He grabbed the vampyr's jaw and twisted his head. 'You live at her sufferance. You owe her debt,' he snarled, then he let the boy go.

The vampyr didn't look back. He ran off, faster than

Usain Bolt.

'Fast, isn't he?' I commented.

'So are rats,' Emory grunted.

'Not a big vampyr fan?' I asked.

'I forget you're new to the realm. Dragons and vampyrs don't get on. Pre-Verdict we'd try to kill each other on sight. We're both immortals in that we don't die of natural causes, so we're both keen on instigating unnatural causes in the other species. No one really remembers how our feud started but it is as old as the sun. Hatred of their race is steeped in our bones, and they have whole clans dedicated to dragon slaying. Wokeshire isn't one of them,' he sneered, nudging the piles of ash around us.

'Dragons live a peaceful solitary life, gathering wealth,' he continued. 'It's an easy payday for a vampyr clan to kill a dragon – a dragon's hoard can keep a clan wealthy for years. If Conrad's home had been divested of his valuables then I would have suspected them, but he had no marks on him and his wealth remained.'

'It looks like I'd better visit Wokeshire without you,' I commented.

He stared at me. 'They just tried to kill you, and you're going to stroll into their clan and ask nicely that they stop?'

'Not just me,' I said rolling my eyes. 'That'd be stupid.' I hauled out my phone and dialled Nate's number.

'Jinx,' he answered. 'Are you okay?' I could feel his concern, which was quite touching. Apart from being linked by some sort of mental bond we didn't know each other all that well, so it was nice that he cared, even if it only stemmed from a selfish concern that we didn't know what would happen to him if something happened to me. For that reason, we'd kept the bond quiet. Only Nate, his dad Lord Gabriel Volderiss and I knew about it. And I guess Gato did too, since I had no secrets from him.

'I'm fine,' I answered casually. 'How are you?'

'I'm getting a flight home. You've been in danger twice and I haven't been there to protect you.'

'It's not your job to protect me,' I pointed out.

He didn't argue with me, but I felt that he disagreed strongly.

'I've got a dragon protecting me right now,' I admitted, mostly to see what response I'd feel from Nate.

'Dragons are useless at combat,' he snorted. 'That's not reassuring at all.'

'We killed four vampyrs pretty easily.'

'Which clan?'

'Wokeshire.'

'*Wokeshire* attacked you?'

'Yes – is that important?' I asked.

'They're supposed to be in negotiations with my father. If they've gone after you, their negotiations with Father might not be what they seem. Everyone knows you're under Volderiss's protection.'

'I am?'

'Where are you staying?' Nate asked.

I could feel that all he wanted to do was protect me. If it hadn't been for that I'd have hesitated, but instead I rattled off Lucy's address.

'All right. I'm sending a cohort of vampyrs to your location. They should be there within four hours. Sit tight. I'll ring my father and notify him. And I'm booking that flight.' He rang off before I could object.

I turned to Emory. 'Vampyr politics can get a bit murky.'

'Apparently so. Let's head back. We've learnt all we can for now.'

We fell into silence on the walk to the car. I didn't know what Emory was thinking, but my brain was catching up with the attack, and I was feeling a little outraged.

At the car, I beeped open my boot and pulled out my bag of baby wipes. They were mostly there to wipe up Gato's slobber but, in a pinch, they'd be handy to wipe the blood off me.

I opened the door, slid inside and turned on the lights. When I flipped down the vanity mirror, I let out a shriek. I looked like an extra from a horror movie. There was blood everywhere.

My leather jacket was fairly easily fixed; it still had

holes in it from Archie's teeth but at least the blood would wipe off. My white shirt was ruined; no amount of Vanish was going to save that. I looked dubiously at the baby wipes in my hand; they just weren't going to cut it.

Emory looked immaculate. 'How come you're not covered in blood?' I asked plaintively.

'It doesn't seem to survive the transformation. I always shift back to my clothes as they were beforehand. They weren't blood soaked then, so they're not now.'

'That's handy,' I muttered a tad sullenly. I couldn't turn up to Lucy's in this shirt. Dammit, I really needed to start carrying spare clothes in the boot like Stone did.

I shrugged off my jacket and gave it a quick wipe down. I could feel the weight of Glimmer in the pocket. I looked down at my bloody shirt and bit my lip. Emory wasn't smiling though he looked distinctly amused. He shrugged out of his suit jacket and started to undo his own shirt.

'What are you doing?' I asked, a little alarmed.

He sent me a smirk. 'Lending you my far cleaner shirt.'

'Oh.' I paused. 'That's very kind of you. Thank you.'

I swear the temperature in the car ratcheted up a couple of degrees as he undid his shirt. He was *cut*. His muscles had muscles; he was like an Abercrombie and Fitch model. I tried to make sure there was no visible drool. I mean, the last abs I'd seen were Stone's in a hotel room in the Lake District, and that had been lovely but disappointingly platonic.

As Emory passed me his shirt, it took a few moments for me to tear my gaze away from his torso. 'Uh, thanks,' I stuttered eloquently.

'My pleasure,' he purred. He turned his full attention on me. Uh-oh. This strip show was not going to be as sexy. I'd had a big breakfast that morning, and I was sitting down; there were going to be rolls. And more rolls.

I met Emory's gaze and must have looked panicked because he laughed softly. 'I won't bite,' he teased. Nevertheless, he shifted his body so he was facing his own door, giving me some semblance of privacy.

'Thanks,' I muttered again and made quick work of peeling off my filthy shirt. My white lace bra was also ruined. I gave it a futile clean. Then I gave my skin a quick once over with the wipes, then pulled on Emory's shirt. It was like clothing my body in heaven. Who knew expensive shirts felt so nice? And smelled so good. Sandalwood and spice and something male and nice... Yum.

I buttoned up the shirt and wiped my face. 'Okay,' I said, 'I'm all decent.'

'I'm not,' Emory admitted with a hot glance.

'Erm...'

He laughed and shrugged on his suit jacket. You could still see all of those delicious abs but at least he was semi-clothed, like an expensive stripper. He was definitely my kind of strippergram.

Emory pulled another wipe out of the pack and leaned over to me. 'You've still got a little bit here,' he said as he gently wiped something off my ear. I swallowed hard. Never has removing blood been so sexy. He was close enough for me to feel his breath. 'All clean,' he murmured.

'Thanks,' I said tightly as he sat back. 'Belt up.'

I started the car engine. My sense of self-preservation was kicking in: danger, danger. Quick, distract the sexy dragon with songs. I turned on the radio, switched to a loud rock station and drove us to Lucy's.

CHAPTER 15

I PULLED UP outside Lucy's and looked dubiously at my shirtless guest. The Wokeshire vampyrs were almost certainly after me rather than Emory, but it seemed churlish to send him off on his own. How strong were his brethren? Could they protect him while he was sleeping? I wasn't so sure about my abilities to protect him, but I was confident in Gato's. And besides, I was fairly sure that Emory was Liverpool based, and he probably wouldn't want to stay in the empty desolation of Conrad's mansion. Apart from staying with me, his only other option was probably a hotel.

'Do you want to come in, or should I drop you somewhere else?' I probably should have asked that question before I'd driven him all the way to Lucy's, but my brain had been switched off by the abs.

'That's very kind of you. I'll stay here,' he said easily. 'Thanks.'

'Erm, it's my friend Lucy's house. She's Common.' That felt like a harsh statement to say; there was nothing common about Lucy, save for her realm.

'No problem.' Emory smiled. 'I can mingle.'

I glanced at him dubiously but got out of the car anyway. I knocked on the door and Lucy answered. She was dressed to head out, and she looked annoyed. 'You didn't even text!' she snapped. Then she caught sight of shirtless Emory. 'Never mind,' she murmured, her annoyance melting away. 'I can see why.'

My face was hot. 'Is it okay if Emory stays the night? In your other spare room, I mean?'

'He can stay in whichever room he likes.' Lucy grinned at me. Man, she was embarrassing. 'I was just going to ring you. I'm heading over to James's. Do you mind? I wouldn't have left Gato.'

I felt instantly contrite. 'Ah, I'm sorry Luce, you should have gone. Gato would have been fine by himself.'

Lucy cast my hound a sidelong glance. 'Yeah. Oddly enough, I swear that's what he was trying to tell me.' She shook her head as if to rid herself of foolish flights of fancy and grabbed an overnight bag by the front door. 'I cooked lasagne for dinner. There's plenty left. And some wine too.' She gave me a quick air kiss. 'Do him,' she whispered.

'Luce!' I said in strangled voice. God, I hoped dragons had shit hearing. 'Get out!'

She laughed and squeezed me. 'Lovely to meet you, Emory.'

'Thank you for letting me stay,' Emory responded

with a friendly smile. He sat down casually onto the sofa.

Lucy waved and shut the door behind her. Once it was closed, Gato came over and sniffed me. He let out a low growl. 'Vampyrs,' I confirmed. 'Wokeshire, apparently.'

Gato turned to Emory, and the growl increased in volume. His spikes stood up and he grew into his Battle Cat form. 'Hey!' I objected. 'He's a friendly dragon!'

Emory smirked. 'No I'm not. I'm the Prime and your hound knows it.'

Gato stalked over, eyes red and spikes quivering. He stood in front of Emory, towering over him. Emory lounged back into the sofa, met Gato's eyes and held them. They must have stayed like that for more than three minutes, neither of them blinking.

'Oh for goodness' sake,' I muttered. They could play staring competitions if they wanted to but I wanted a shower. I left them to it.

After my shower I hesitated. My usual nightclothes were tiny shorts and a tank top. Prancing around in next to nothing didn't seem like a good idea. I pulled on Mrs Dawes' nightdress; it was an effective passion killer. Then I stared at myself in the mirror. Was I really going to let possibly the sexiest man alive see me in this? I blew out a sharp breath. Yup.

I went down to the kitchen and started warming the lasagne in the microwave. Emory heard the noise and joined me. He must have resolved the great stare-down because Gato followed him in Great Dane form.

'Who won?' I asked as I poured myself a glass of wine.

Emory stopped dead as he took in my nightdress then let out an unbelieving laugh. He met my eyes with a warm smile. 'Just so you know, that's not enough to stop me.' He reached over and poured wine for himself. 'I think your best friend gives good advice.'

I blushed furiously. Right: dragons have good hearing. Good to know. 'Lasagne?' I offered, flustered.

'Sure.' He was enjoying himself.

He sat at Lucy's breakfast bar. He was still only wearing a suit jacket and trousers, and it was distracting. 'I'll grab your shirt,' I offered lamely.

'No hurry, I'm warm enough.'

'I bet you are,' I muttered under my breath. Shit! I looked up and met his eyes. Now he was openly grinning at me.

'Shit. Shirt!' I blurted and bolted for the stairs.

In the bedroom, I gave myself a talking-to in the mirror – silently, in case Emory had *really* good hearing. *Right, Jinx, he's sexy but you don't know him and you're not that kind of girl. Settle down. Anyway, he's kind of a client.*

I was halfway down the stairs before I realised I'd forgotten his shirt. I went back up to get it. By the time I returned to the kitchen, Emory had taken off his suit jacket and slung it over the back of the barstool. 'Jackets aren't that comfortable,' he said. *True.*

I handed him his shirt and he gamely put it on and did up a token button or two.

'More buttons,' I ordered and glared at him.

His eyes were laughing. 'Sure thing.' He did up two more.

I poured myself some more wine. 'Tell me about dragons,' I said as I sat down with my lasagne. His plate was clean, which made me wonder how long I'd been giving myself a pep talk for.

'What do you want to know?' he asked, sipping his wine.

Do dragons have pheromones that make them super sexy, or is that just you? 'Anything you want to tell me.' I cleared my throat. 'Anything I should know. I mean, you're not going to transform into a dragon and wreck Lucy's house when you're sleeping, right?'

'Right,' he agreed. 'I only do intentional transformations, like the wolves.'

'For the wolves, the transformation is—' I stopped myself before I said pleasurable. 'Pain free,' I substituted. 'Is it pain free for you?'

He nodded. 'Dragon and human forms are both inherent to us, so changing is like slipping on a night gown. Or taking it off. The way we appear is just like a set of clothes.'

'Do you prefer being in dragon form?'

He shrugged. 'I'm a dragon, regardless of the form I'm in. Flying is amazing, but the human form has its advantages.'

There was something that made me think he wanted me to ask what. Like a fool, I did. 'What advantages?'

He smiled. 'Human hands and tongues have far greater dexterity.'

I blushed. Why did I have to ask? I cleared my throat. 'Your plate's empty. Do you want some more food? Do dragons eat more than humans?'

'We do,' he admitted. 'I'll have a little more please. Cold is fine.'

I gave him a look of abject horror. 'Serve you cold lasagne? Lucy wouldn't let me stay again if that's how I represented her hospitality.' There was still a sizeable piece of lasagne left, and I put it in the microwave. We'd see how much he needed to eat.

I watched, genuinely impressed, as he put it all away with very little effort. I looked around the kitchen. There was a bag of crisps and some fruit. 'Crisps? Fruit?'

'How about we share the crisps while we watch a movie and wait for your vampyrs to come?'

'They're not *my* vampyrs. They're just vampyrs that apparently will protect me.'

'Sure. That's different.'

'Completely different,' I agreed, ignoring his heavy sarcasm.

We put on the TV and flipped through a few channels until I found an action movie. Emory sat beside me. He wasn't too close – but he'd ignored the other sofa and chosen to sit next to me.

'Action movie?' I queried.

'Sounds good.'

It was fast paced with a lot of explosions and a fair amount of gunfire. I could have done with fewer sex scenes. The tension was palpable – at least to me.

The doorbell rang. 'Oh, thank God,' I muttered, leaping off the sofa to open the door. In my haste, I forgot what I was wearing.

I opened the door. There was a crowd of vampyrs on Lucy's doorstep, chief of whom appeared to be Volderiss's secretary, Verona.

'What are you doing here?' I asked incredulously. Verona is icy blonde and paler than Wilf. Her stunning blue eyes shine and her lips are always blood red. She was dressed in black leather trousers, a corset and a leather jacket.

'Saving your pathetic ass, apparently,' she spat. Then she looked me up and down and sniggered. 'What the hell are you wearing?'

My cheeks warmed but I played it out. I rolled my eyes. 'Better than dressing like Dominatrix Vampyr

Barbie. Could you be any more clichéd?' There was a time when I first joined the Other realm that I was afraid of vampyrs, but they couldn't enter Lucy's home without an invitation, so I wasn't afraid of Verona. It probably wasn't wise to taunt her, but she brought out the worst in me.

'Better a cliché than that abomination!' She gestured at my nightdress. 'At least I'm sexy.'

'Jinx is sexy.' Emory emerged from the living room and leaned casually against the front door.

'Dragon,' Verona hissed, baring her fangs. The vampyrs around her tensed and jostled, fangs out.

'My dragon,' I said firmly. 'He's my guest and if you even *think* about harming one hair on his head, I'll sic Nate on you.'

Verona subsided with effort, nostrils still flared, eyes a little wild. 'Fine. We have instructions to guard you through the night. Tomorrow afternoon, when the Wokeshire cohort are at their weakest, we'll take you to their lord – with an appropriate escort.'

She stepped back, keeping her eyes on Emory. The vampyrs beside her moved into the shadows and melted out of sight. Neat trick. Verona leaned against a lamp-post. I guessed we were done talking.

I shut the front door and locked it. 'Gato?' I called. He came downstairs. 'Were you sleeping on Lucy's bed? You know you're not allowed to do that. Do you need to go out?' He wagged an affirmative, and I let him do his business in the back garden.

I yawned. It was late, time for bed. I locked the door when Gato was done. Emory was waiting patiently. 'Do you need anything?' I asked. 'I think Lucy has a new toothbrush under the sink in her bathroom.'

'Could I have a glass of water?'

'Sure.' I grabbed us both a pint, and we headed upstairs. 'This is your room,' I said abruptly to Emory, gesturing to the third bedroom. 'Night.'

'Good night, Jinx. See you in the morning.' He sent me a sexy smile, which I did my best to ignore. I cleared my throat.

I nodded goodnight since words temporarily escaped me, and Gato and I went into the second bedroom. It had a Jack-and-Jill en-suite that it shared with Lucy's room. I brushed my teeth and settled into bed.

In the darkness of the night, I covered my head with a pillow and groaned as I remembered calling Emory, the prime dragon, 'my dragon'. Uggghhhh. I was so embarrassing.

With some effort, I started my meditative exercises. My mum had always been compulsive about mindfulness. I started my breathing exercises and imagined the beach. Before I had walked to the waves, I was asleep.

CHAPTER 16

I SLEPT WELL and woke clear headed. No sign of a hangover, thank goodness, probably because of all the food I'd eaten. I showered and dressed in some ripped jeans and a T-shirt; I didn't want to inadvertently show Lord Wokeshire any respect, so scrappy clothes it was.

Lucy's house was quiet. It was a Saturday morning, and I guessed she was having a lazy morning with her boyfriend, James. Good for her.

I let Gato out and raided the fridge. The sausages and bacon were still there, and meat seemed like a good choice for a dragon's breakfast. Normally I'd do a couple of rashers of bacon and a couple of sausages per person but, remembering how much lasagne Emory had tucked away the previous night, I decided I'd better do both full packs. I put in a few rounds of bread to toast and set the kettle to boil. I needed a brew. I'm a tea girl except if I'm working; then it's coffee time.

'Good morning, Jinx,' Emory greeted me. 'I trust you slept well.'

'Morning, Mr Prime,' I sassed back.

His lips twitched. 'Just Prime will do, or you can call me Prime Elite, if you prefer.'

'I'd better not – you'd get big headed. I made you breakfast. Lots of breakfast. I hope you're hungry. Are you a tea or coffee man?'

'Both,' he said easily. 'I'll have whatever you're having.'

I made us both a cup of tea. 'Hey,' I objected, 'where's the suit?'

Emory was dressed in dark jeans and a grey V-necked T-shirt. I couldn't decide if he looked better in the suit or in the casual clothes.

'I had some of the brethren bring by some things this morning.' He sipped his tea as we both loaded up our plates. I was gratified to see he was planning to eat everything I'd cooked. We ate our breakfast in companionable silence for a while.

Finally Emory asked, 'What are our plans today?'

'*Our* plans?'

'*Our* plans. You seem to have a knack for getting into the thick of it. That's where I need to be.'

'I don't normally take my clients out with me,' I pointed out.

He shrugged. 'The customer is always right. You're taking me.' He was clearly used to being obeyed. His voice was flat: this wasn't a suggestion, it was an order.

I don't usually react well to orders but I recognised

the futility of arguing. I could stamp my foot and protest but he was going to come anyway, whether it was trailing behind me or standing next to me. 'Fine. I have a personal errand this morning. It probably won't fit with the case, so you can have the morning off.'

'You got attacked last night. I'll come with you on the errand.'

I blew out a breath. 'How well do you get on with werewolves?'

'We get along well enough, considering they're on the human side of things. Ultimately we're both shifter species.'

'Okay, I guess you can come with.'

'Thank you for your kind permission,' he said dryly. I was amusing him again.

I filled the sink with hot water and started to wash the dishes. My jaw dropped a little when Emory picked up a tea towel and dried them. 'The dragon king does the dishes?'

'Not normally,' he admitted. 'But I'm trying to make a good impression. How am I doing?'

'Great,' I admitted before my brain could catch up to my mouth.

He winked. 'Worth it then.' He picked up another plate.

If there is a sexier sight than a man doing dishes, I don't know what it is.

After we'd finished, I did a quick tidy of the house and we headed out. I grabbed my trusty bum bag and slung it on. Today it contained a sachet of Boost and my lockpicking tools. I didn't want to leave either of those at Lucy's.

The vampyrs were still outside. 'We're going to Lord Samuel's,' I explained and they piled into their cars.

As I went to beep open my car, Emory chucked me a set of keys. 'You can drive mine,' he suggested, pointing at the shiny black Mercedes G Wagon AMG parked next to my Ford Focus.

'Oh my God!' I squealed and took a step towards the 150,000 pound car before glancing down at Gato. 'Do you mind if he comes in the car?'

'Not at all,' he reassured me. 'Gato and I have reached an accord.'

I was more concerned about the dog smell than the fear of imminent attack, but I wasn't going to argue – I was going to drive this bad boy! I hopped in. The car had that new car smell, and the inside was all leather seats and luxury. I was in car heaven. One day an Audi, another day a Merc. I'd obviously been a good girl in a past life.

'You sure you're okay with me driving?' I asked as I adjusted the seat and mirrors. I was asking just to be polite; in truth, he'd have had to shoehorn me out of the car.

'Definitely. I don't drive.'

I turned to him. 'What do you mean you don't drive?'

'I don't have a licence. I haven't bothered learning yet. Cars are still pretty new.'

'Cars have been around for 110 years or so,' I pointed out.

'Yeah,' he agreed. 'New.'

My eyes widened. 'How old *are* you?'

He didn't answer and turned on the radio. Huh.

I drove on autopilot to Wilf's. I wasn't looking forward to this meeting. I'd texted Amber DeLea the previous night and asked her to remove my mind clearance. She'd agreed and suggested meeting somewhere neutral like Wilf's. She'd said I might feel a little disorientated afterwards, so I didn't want her to do it somewhere public like Rosie's. Wilf had agreed readily enough, and I'd contacted him this morning to give him a heads up about my vampyric guards. He'd sent me an emoji thumbs up; I inferred from that that he wasn't bothered about undead escorts.

I drew up on the gravel drive and parked. The two cars full of vampyrs parked up behind me but they didn't get out. I guess they knew I was safe at Wilf's.

Mrs Dawes opened the door with a wide smile, which faltered a little at the sight of Emory. When I was bleeding and Archie was naked she hadn't batted an eyelid, but a dragon was a surprise?

She blinked rapidly before giving Emory a bow. 'Jinx,

you brought … a friend. How nice. Come in. I'll let Lord Samuel know you're here. He's just having a chat with Miss DeLea in the breakfast room.'

She stowed us in the main reception room and bustled off to fetch Wilf. Emory sat on one of the couches; he looked indolent, like Archie. I rolled my eyes. 'Don't sprawl on other people's furniture,' I chastened.

He grinned. 'You have all these rules.' Nevertheless, he straightened up.

Wilf came in with Amber. 'Prime,' he acknowledged coolly, inclining his head. No bowing from Wilf but no rudeness either, just oodles of tempered caution.

Amber curtseyed. 'Prime,' she said, her tone respectful and far friendlier than anything I'd heard from her so far.

Emory nodded to them both in acknowledgement but did not stand. 'Miss DeLea, Lord Samuel.'

Amber turned to me, all business; all hints of friendliness had gone. 'Breaking a clearing hurts,' she warned. 'Are you sure you need this memory back?'

I wasn't, but I needed to know who had cleared me – was it a friend or foe?

'Yes,' I said.

'Sit down then.' Amber reached into her ever-present black tote bag and pulled out a jar filled with black sludge. It looked vile, and I hoped I wasn't going to have to consume it. She pulled on her disposable gloves, purple this time, and got a paintbrush out of her bag. She carefully dipped the brush into the sludge and started painting on my forehead.

The moment her brush touched my head, flashes started to come to me.

Gato pulling me back with his teeth. Guard unicorns instead of hounds. A dragon roaring overhead. It was the night I broke into Conrad's house. As Amber painted, filling in the triangles on my forehead, the memories came thicker and faster, more vivid than any memories I'd ever had.

I could smell the scent of the grass, hear the crunch of my feet on the gravel that I tried to silence. I could sense the roar of my heartbeat and the rush of blood in my ears as I tried to escape with the vase. And finally, *finally* – a knock at the door of my house.

An old man was standing there, but this time I knew him. Leo Harfen, older than when I'd met him, but there was no doubting it was that tricksy elf. He cleared my mind. Then I saw Wilf's arrival and his forlorn look as he realised I'd been cleared. He'd been genuinely devastated.

I blinked several times and then I was back in the room. Amber was watching me curiously. 'You should be screaming,' she commented, raising an eyebrow. 'Do you have any seer blood in your family?'

Not in my family but in my own blood. Several weeks earlier I had used Glimmer to cut myself; as I did so, I'd received Mrs H's seer magic. To my knowledge it had done absolutely nothing for me except to allow me to destroy her protective field.

'Something like that,' I said vaguely.

I wasn't a touchy-feely person, but Wilf's upset had resonated deeply with me; he really did care about me. I didn't have many people in my life who did. I stepped close to him and hugged him. His arms encircled me immediately, warm and comforting. 'I'm sorry he wiped me,' I said softly. 'You were upset.'

'Yes,' he admitted. He kissed me softly on my forehead, and it felt fatherly and caring. It was nice to be cared about. Wilf had been watching over me, trying to get me introduced, for years.

'Thanks, Wilf.'

His arms tightened around me. 'No problem,' he said lightly. *Lie.* He'd gambled a multi-million-pound vase to give me an excuse to prowl around a dragon's lair so Gato would portal me. Yes, Wilf had gone to quite some lengths to help me.

I let myself enjoy the hug a moment longer; it was a long while since anyone other than Lucy and Mrs Dawes had hugged me properly. Well, Stone had, but I tried to think about that as little as possible. I'd forgotten how nice hugs were.

I stepped back and turned to Amber. 'Thanks. Invoice me,' I said.

Wilf shook his head. 'Invoice me.'

Emory waved us both away. 'Invoice me.'

I grinned. 'No, I'm Spartacus.'

Amber observed us coolly. 'I'm more than happy to invoice all three of you.' She packed her bag, her eyes lingering on Gato, then she nodded to my dog and left.

'Where's Archie?' I asked curiously.

'He's in the gym,' Wilf replied, a touch of pride in his voice.

'Really? Normally he's lounging around at this time of day.'

'He's a new wolf since the battle – since his blooding.'

'He was pretty proud of his rank,' I commented.

Wilf smiled. 'As he should be.' His chest puffed out with pride.

'I'm sorry I missed him.' I was surprised to find that was true. 'I've got another appointment. Tell him I said hi.'

Wilf saw us out. He looked at the cars full of vampyrs. 'Be careful, Jinx. Wokeshire has been increasingly … erratic this last year. Don't mouth off.'

'Who? Me?' I gave him an innocent smile and made no promises.

I climbed into Emory's car and hauled out my phone before I started the engine. I dialled Leo Harfen, the number on his white business card still fresh in my mind. It went straight to voicemail. 'It's Jinx,' I said. 'Call me, you interfering old elf.'

CHAPTER 17

'ONE MORE ERRAND,' I explained to Emory. 'Sorry.'

He shrugged. 'I've cleared my diary for the next few days. I promised Conrad's mother I'd find the one who is ultimately responsible for his death.'

I understood. Conrad had been young and impetuous, and he'd willingly taken the drugs that had ended his life, but he never would have done so if he'd known that they could kill him. Boost was deadly, like playing Russian roulette; you could end up high or dead.

As I started the car engine, my phone rang. It was an unknown number. The car's Bluetooth system picked it up and the screen gave me the option to answer hands free. I touched yes and a voice filled the car.

'Jinx. I trust the vampyrs made the situation clear to you. Stop digging into Reggie's death, or you'll be joining him in the morgue.' The voice was low and distorted. It should have been scary and threatening, but I'd seen too many bad horror films to find it anything more than amusing.

'And you are?' I enquired.

'The one who will order your death. This is none of your concern. Go back to following cheating husbands.'

'The wives cheat a fair bit too,' I sassed.

'Stop your investigation or die.' The caller wasn't happy that I wasn't taking him seriously.

Emory was taking him seriously enough for both of us. His green eyes were narrowed and his jaw was tight as he took the phone from me. 'Jinx is under my protection. You come after her, and I will raze your holdings to the ground.' *True.*

Wasn't that sweet? Some girls like flowers and chocolate; nothing melts my heart more than a threat of arson.

'Stay out of this, Prime. This doesn't concern you,' the voice snarled.

'One of mine is dead,' Emory growled viciously.

'That was … unfortunate. I assure you that no more dragons will be involved. I consider that the end of the matter.' *True.*

'I do not,' Emory retorted and he cut off the call.

I drove the car slowly down the drive. 'Well,' I said brightly, 'we're on the right track. You know you're getting close when you start getting threats.'

Emory smiled and the atmosphere lightened. 'You're pretty unshakeable. Has anyone ever told you that?'

My smile dimmed. Stone had commented on it a time or two. 'Yeah,' I sighed. 'Apparently so.'

I turned on the music and concentrated on driving

that beautiful piece of machinery. The engine purred and roared in turn as we glided off to Slough with two cars of vampyrs following on behind.

Someone once wrote a poem about Slough, about how it should be bombed off the face of the planet. I feel that's a little harsh; I was born there, and I feel a certain connection to the area. Okay, so crime rates are a little on the high side but nowhere is perfect.

Mo lived on the cusp of a nice area and a fairly rough council estate. By day he was an IT technician; by night and on weekends, he hacked computers and anything else you paid him well for.

I drew up outside his house. The area was downmarket, but with a Merc as our car of choice, everyone would assume we were drug dealers. They'd leave it well alone. Anyway, we wouldn't be out of it for long. Mo never let business into his house; for all I knew, he had four kids and a dog in there.

I let Gato out of the boot so he could have a wee and a stretch. When it became clear we were at our destination, the vampyrs decamped from their cars and spread out. Verona wasn't there, so I guessed they'd changed shifts. Just how many had Volderiss sent?

I knocked on the door and there was a pause before it was opened. Today Mo was in a white shirt and jeans, weekend business casual. The white shirt made his dark skin pop. As always, he looked good.

He looked at my entourage, and his gaze settled on Emory for a long moment. 'You expanding your crew?' he asked sardonically.

'Something like that.' I smiled but didn't elaborate. 'Is the laptop ready?' I asked the question to move matters along; I knew full well that it was because he'd texted last night to say so.

Mo nodded and closed the front door. He re-emerged a moment later with the laptop in a black plastic bag.

'You should switch to canvas bags,' I suggested. 'They're better for the environment.'

'I'll take that under advisement,' Mo said lightly. *Lie.* He was not going to swap to canvas bags.

'We've only got one planet,' I pointed out. Probably – unless the realms were on spatially different planets. I slid a glance at Emory, who shook his head and looked amused. Okay, definitely only one planet.

I had a roll of cash in my jeans pocket. I dug it out and chucked it to Mo. 'Thanks,' I said. 'Anything of interest?'

'I don't look, you know that. I never see anything.' *Lie.*

I rolled my eyes. 'Yeah, yeah. Okay, cheers, Mo.'

'Until next time, Jinx.' He glanced again at my protective detail and went to shut the door.

'Wait!' I called. I stepped closer to him and lowered my voice. 'You heard anything about a new drug hitting the streets?'

His face blanked instantly, and he shrugged one shoulder. 'There's always a new drug.'

'This one is called Boost.'

There was silence. 'I've heard of it,' he said finally. 'Apparently it's very pricey and very exclusive. The dealers have their own criteria for who they sell it to – and money alone isn't enough. The streets are all talking about it, they call it the drug the dealers don't want to sell. It makes everyone want it more, and prices are sky high – more than you gave me in that roll for a single gram.'

'You heard anything about it being deadly?'

He frowned. 'No. Is it?'

'To some,' I said. 'That's why they're picky about who they sell it to. They don't want too many deaths because it's bad publicity, but the odd one occurs.'

His frown deepened. 'I'll tug some lines.'

'Be careful. These guys aren't boy scouts.'

'Neither am I.' Mo nodded dismissively and this time I let him shut the door.

Boost had leaked through into the Common realm. There had never been an Other drug there before, only Common ones. What would an Other drug do to someone with no power to boost?

I bit my lip. Maybe it was time to ring Steve again. But first, the laptop was calling to me. Reggie wouldn't have changed the passwords for no reason; there was something on it. And I wanted to see what it was.

Once again we all piled into the cars. I didn't want to take this parade back to Lucy's, so I headed to Rosie's instead. Hey, a girl needs to eat.

Emory didn't comment on my decision about a lunch venue. The vampyrs remained outside once again while Emory and I went inside. I'd had a big breakfast but I was still peckish, so I ordered a salmon-and-egg salad with a chai latte and a side of chocolate brownie. Emory went for another full breakfast. He paid for both of us while I slid into what I was beginning to consider my usual booth. Emory sat next to me rather than opposite – I guess he wanted to see the laptop's contents too.

I made sure it was at an angle so that no one else could see its contents, then I turned it on. Mo had removed the password protection screen and the computer was unlocked; I knew he would have unlocked any files with passwords too. The computer was my oyster.

The screensaver was an image of Reggie with Joyce and their two children, Wren and Rose. It tugged my heart strings. At that moment, they'd been a happy family; those children would never have a moment like that again. I should know: missing my parents is a hollow ache in my chest that never quite fades. Sometimes, like at that moment, grief at their loss kicked me when I wasn't expecting it. I had no idea what my parents would think of my life choices. My dad would never walk me down the aisle; Rose and Wren's dad would never do that with them either. Even worse, Wren wouldn't have a single memory to cling to.

I often feel bitter about my loss. My parents were too young to die, and I was too young to lose them. But I had eighteen years with them, eighteen years of being loved and looked after, and I try to be grateful for that. It's better than a lot of people get. But the bitterness remains. One day acceptance might come, but I'm still waiting for that day to arrive.

I'd been staring at the image too long. Emory nudged my shoulder lightly. 'Did you know him?' he asked gently.

'No, but I know his wife and his kids slightly. That picture kicks up old dirt. My parents died when I was young.'

'I'm sorry,' Emory said softly, giving my hand a squeeze.

'Those kids won't have a dad.'

'They'll have a mum,' he pointed out gently.

'Yeah. That's better than nothing, I guess.'

Emory nodded; his face held something that made me think he knew something about having nothing.

I focused back on the laptop and pushed my emotional baggage to one side. I'd deal with it another time, a better time – like never.

I started opening the folders on the screen. The one of pictures had nothing but images of Reggie and his family; nothing untoward there. Another folder, labelled work, contained files from his time at Wright Freeth and Sykes. I diligently looked through them all, but nothing stood out. If I got desperate, maybe I could ask Lucy to examine them; she's an accountant, so she might have a better eye for something hinky.

The next folder was entitled Miller. I clicked on it and entered a sub-folder entitled pictures. There were a lot of photos showing Fred Miller, the Fredster, dealing little pink baggies to kids outside a school. So this was what Mo had found.

Reggie was a family man; he may have slipped from a righteous path, but I didn't get the vibe from those that knew him that he'd be okay with selling drugs to kids. In fact, the very existence of the photos suggested he *wasn't* okay with it.

I clicked onto his emails. His inbox was full of the usual spam, so I clicked onto the sent items. There it was, in black and white: an email sent to Inspector Stone.

Stone

My wife met with you recently. She is not a fan of the Connection, but she was impressed by you. She said you weren't what she'd expected. I trust my wife's judgment in all things.

I need your help. I'm in too deep. I've gone too far, and I can't get out. They're dealing Boost to kids. For some, it boosts your power, gives you a rush; for others, that boost is too big, and it kills you. Nobody knows what causes one reaction or the other, but it hasn't stopped them selling it.

They're working on something else, too, something monstrous that's going to change everything. It mustn't be allowed. I know all the players. We can bring this down – we <u>need</u> to bring this down.

I want witness protection for me and my family, and immunity for my crimes. Then I'll tell you everything – and, believe me, you need to hear it for the sake of the Verdict.

Reggie Evergreen.

It was sent one day after Fred Miller's death. Miller had been killed by a branch in the chest, something a dryad could manage easily. I would bet my life savings that Reggie Evergreen had gone vigilante.

CHAPTER 18

T HE REST OF the laptop held very little of interest save for one final Word document on the desktop entitled 'Dear R'. I clicked on the properties; it had been created and saved ten days earlier, shortly before Reggie's death. It read simply, *'Dear R – I can't keep doing this. I love you. I'm sorry.'*

My first thought was that it was a message from Joyce. You should always look at the spouse when there's a murder – that's PI Class 101. I had dismissed Joyce from the picture early on because I liked her, and besides she'd hired me. But she wouldn't be the first murderer to hire a PI to muddy the waters and to provide a smokescreen.

Could Joyce Evergreen really be as ignorant as she appeared? Her husband had been working for drug dealers, and she'd supposedly had no idea. There had to have been late-night meetings, unexplained income. There must have been plenty of red flags that Reggie was up to something.

My gut didn't like it but that's where the facts were

telling me to look. Joyce had access to the laptop, even though she denied knowing the passwords. She could easily have left this message for Reggie to find. And then what? Hired a professional killer? But why leave the note?

I chewed on my bottom lip. I didn't like it, but Joyce needed to be my next port of call. And then Elvira, since Stone wasn't answering my calls. If Reggie had made contact with the Connection as his email indicated, why hadn't he been placed in witness protection?

There were too many unknowns. I still felt that drugs were the answer to it all – drugs or someone who'd found out that Fred Miller's death was no accident. I tapped out a text to Steve Marley, asking if he could find out about Fred's next of kin. Maybe there was a sister or mother who had hired a griffin as revenge – it was hard to see the Fredster as someone who had a wife.

I got an immediate reply from Steve, saying he'd let me know what he found out. I didn't tell him my suspicions about Reggie. Reggie was dead; it didn't seem necessary to drag his name, and Joyce's, through the mud of an investigation. Thanks to the rogue witch's enchantment, the cops had ruled Miller's death an accident. For now, I was leaving it at that. Some might think my moral code is fast and loose but I have my own set of rules that I live by, and this felt right to me.

I rang Joyce and asked if I could swing by. She said she was just putting down Wren for her afternoon nap.

Rose was at pre-school, so now would be fine. I told her I was fifteen minutes away.

Emory and I climbed into the car and set off with the motorcade following behind. My dragon friend was quiet, watching me as I drove. 'You're thinking the spouse,' he said suddenly.

I shook my head. 'No, I don't think so, but I need to cross her off. It's time to tell her some home truths and see how she reacts.'

'Ah yes, your empathy,' he mused. 'How strongly can you feel someone's emotions?'

I shrugged. 'I haven't been trained in it. Sometimes I can feel it like it's my own, sometimes not a whisper. I should probably get a book or something on how to do it.'

'I think it's something you need to have proper tutelage in, not just a textbook.'

'I don't know many people in the Other yet,' I admitted. 'Certainly not anyone who openly admits to being an empath.'

'It's rare,' Emory confirmed. 'But I know one. I'll see if she's willing to help.' He got out his phone and sent a text. 'So your empathy might not help us at all if it's feeling temperamental.'

'I'll still be able to tell if she's telling the truth,' I pointed out.

Emory looked at me sharply. 'You're a truth seeker?'

'Yeah.'

His eyes widened. 'That's not something you want to be widely known.'

'No, apparently not,' I sighed.

'Empaths are rare, truth seekers are almost extinct. I don't know anyone who admits to being a truth seeker.' *True.*

'You always tell the truth,' I said to him. 'Well, you have so far.'

'Yes.' Emory's tone was matter of fact. 'I'm a dragon.'

I blinked. 'So?'

'Dragons can't lie. The closest we can get is being sarcastic, but it has to be really clear we're being sarcastic.'

'You can't lie? Or you just don't?'

'We can't,' he declared.

'What would happen if you did?'

'I have no idea because it's an impossibility. Like the moon coming up in the morning, it just won't happen.'

'Is this widely known?'

Emory nodded. 'Of course. Everyone knows you can always trust a dragon's word.'

'Except if he's being sarcastic.'

He grinned. 'Yeah, except then.'

'That's a weird exception to the rule.'

'Welcome to the Other,' Emory smirked, 'where weird rules supreme.'

I couldn't argue with that. Since coming to the Other, I'd seen a dryad walk into a tree, my dog turn into a hellacious beast and I'd gone back to a funky 1980s' time warp. So yeah, the Other was weird. But I liked it. Finally, it felt like I'd found where I fitted in. It frustrated me that my parents had kept me from it for so long. I had to trust that they'd had a good reason, but they weren't here to tell me what it was.

We drew up outside Joyce's home. Since she had just put Wren down, I texted to say we were there rather than ringing the doorbell. It would be easier to talk to Joyce if her baby stayed asleep.

Joyce got the message and opened the front door. Her eyes widened as she stared at Emory. 'Prime Elite,' she stuttered. 'You honour my home.' She gave him a deep curtsy.

He inclined his head in acknowledgement. 'I'm sorry for your loss,' he said gently.

Joyce's eyes filled up as she motioned us into the house. 'Thank you, Prime. Did you know Reggie?'

Emory shook his head. 'No, I'm afraid not. But his death appears to be linked to a drug that killed one of my dragons.'

'Drug?' she replied, baffled.

'Let's sit,' I suggested, leading the way into the lounge. The walls were a soothing green with thick, mustard-coloured brocade curtains. There were family portraits on every wall.

Joyce sat down then immediately rose again. 'Tea? Coffee?'

I shook my head. 'We've just been to Rosie's. We're fine, thanks.'

Joyce settled back down. Her green skin looked paler than before – she looked exhausted. I felt bad that I wasn't going to help, but it needed to be said. 'As you know, Reggie hadn't been working at Wright Freeth and Sykes for nearly a year.'

Joyce nodded and wrung her hands.

I softened my tone. 'Joyce … it seems that Reggie was working for a drug cartel as their accountant.'

Her mouth dropped open and hung there while she stared at me in total disbelief. After a minute she shut it with a clack and shook her head. 'I'm sorry but you're wrong,' she said firmly. 'Reggie grew up on a terrible estate where people were poorer than poor. He grew up around crime, and he saw what drugs did to people – to kids, to families. He wouldn't. He just wouldn't.'

'What if he didn't have a choice?' I asked.

Her brow furrowed. 'What do you mean?'

'Blackmail,' I suggested. It was the only reason I could think of that someone upstanding would do a U-turn in life. And she was right, Reggie did hate drugs; he hated that Fred Miller had been dealing to kids so much that he'd killed him for it.

She shook her head. 'Reggie didn't have anything to

be blackmailed about.' *True.* Or at least she thought it was true.

'Not as far as you know,' I said mildly.

'I knew Reggie!'

'You didn't know he was working for a drug cartel for a year,' I pointed out. I was trying not to be too harsh, but it needed to be said.

She stared at me for a moment, her eyes wide and her bottom lip trembling, then she shook her head. Her shoulders shook as she started sobbing soundlessly.

Emory nudged my foot.

What? I mouthed to him.

He tilted his head towards her. *Comfort her,* he mouthed back.

I rolled my eyes. Just because I have empathy doesn't mean I'm good at comforting people. In truth, I knew a little of what she was going through. I'd grieved for my parents most of my life, only to discover they were secretly inspectors for the Connection and had hidden an entire realm from me. I know all about discovering the ones you love have hidden lives.

I sighed audibly, shot Emory a reproachful look and went to comfort Joyce. I sat down on the sofa next to her and put my arm around her. Instantly I was assailed with grief and loss so fresh and strong that tears sprang unbidden to my eyes. Amid that grief there was confusion and anger. Reggie had hidden so much from her, and she felt betrayed.

I knew for certain that this was the first time she'd learnt the truth about Reggie. Her innocence had not been play acting, she truly hadn't known. Something in me eased when I accepted that my gut feelings about her had been right; she definitely wasn't involved in whatever Reggie had been up to.

I kept on hugging her. It was difficult having her emotions surging through me, and my eyes remained dry only because I kept blinking rapidly. My throat felt like it had a rock in it.

Finally, Joyce finished crying and the onslaught of her emotions eased. 'I'm sorry,' she said in a small voice. 'This has come as a shock.'

'Yes.' I squeezed her shoulders lightly. 'It's okay.' I moved back next to Emory on the other sofa to give her a little more space, and to help me regain my equilibrium.

Emory took my hand as I sat down next to him and his calm rushed through me. He was certain we were on the right path, and he was pleased we were making headway. I let his steady presence centre me, gave his hand a grateful squeeze and then let go.

Joyce's eyes narrowed suddenly. 'Have you spoken to Ronan? Did he know Reggie was involved with drugs?'

I nodded. 'Yes. I'm sorry.'

'Damn it.' She exhaled. 'He told Ronan and not me. I don't know why I'm surprised, they told each other everything. They grew up together and they only had each other. If Reggie was being blackmailed, Ronan will know about it.'

I nodded. 'Ronan indicated that he believed Reggie was being blackmailed.'

'And he didn't help him?' She was outraged. 'Some friend he was. If he'd helped, told the Connection…'

'It appears that *Reggie* told the Connection. There's an email on his laptop asking Stone for witness protection.'

'Stone?' she said in confusion. 'Reggie hated the Connection. He thought it was full of corruption and nepotism. The Connection is fundamentally anti-creature, no matter what their posters say.'

'Reggie needed help,' I pointed out. 'He was desperate and he wanted to do the right thing.'

Joyce's eyes filled with tears again but there was also relief in them. 'Yes, that was my Reggie. He was trying to do the right thing. That's who he was.' *True.*

It gave her some comfort to know that her husband had tried to stop helping the criminals. I knew now that Joyce wasn't involved, so there was no reason to tell her about Miller, to have her know that her husband had killed. I would keep it to myself, unless it transpired Miller's next of kin or friends had killed Reggie. For now I'd hold my silence. Joyce had already had enough turbulence; there was only so much a person could take.

CHAPTER 19

W E WERE INTO the afternoon and it was shaping up to be a busy day. We had an appointment with Wokeshire at 4 p.m. but first I detoured to High Wycombe. It was time to speak to Ronan again. Maybe he could shed some light on the blackmail material.

He was on the phone when we walked in. He held his finger up in the universal sign for just one minute. 'Okay,' he said, 'you know what needs to be done.' He hung up and smiled at me. 'Sorry about that.'

'No problem,' I replied. 'What needs to be done?'

'Rats,' he responded. 'They need to be exterminated.' *Lie.* 'Killing animals is my least favourite thing about being a piper. I hate meaningless loss of life.' *True.*

I didn't call him on the rats' lie. I was being entirely too nosy.

Ronan caught sight of Gato and straightened. 'A hell hound!' He stood up and approached, but Gato backed away slowly and moved close to my side.

Ronan held up his hands. 'I won't hurt you, boy.' He promised. *True.* 'I've always wanted a hell hound, but they're predisposed to be wary of pipers.' *True.* He cast a wistful glance at Gato and sat back down at his desk.

I cleared my throat. 'I've just spoken to Joyce and told her Reggie was working for a drug cartel.'

Ronan grimaced. When he spoke, his voice was tight. 'I wish you hadn't done that. She deserves to remember him without thinking poorly of his character.' *True*

'I told her that he was going to the Connection, that he was trying to do the right thing.'

Ronan nodded. 'Yeah, that was Reggie. He was always harping on about the right thing.' He shook his head. 'Such a terrible loss of a good man.' He sighed and scrubbed a hand through his hair. *All true.*

He didn't seem surprised in the slightest that Reggie had been intending to go to the Connection. 'You knew he was going to the Connection?' I asked.

Ronan exhaled sharply and pinched the bridge of his nose. 'I knew. We spoke about it. Honestly? I advised against it. We grew up rough, and we knew what drug cartels are capable of. Snitches don't survive.' *True.*

'Snitches get stitches,' I parroted.

He shook his head. 'Snitches get the morgue.' *True.* Heavy stuff.

I changed tack. 'You said you thought he was being blackmailed. Joyce thinks you'll know about what. What did Reggie do?'

Ronan looked around, seemingly weighing up his

options. Finally, he gave a small sigh. 'I guess it doesn't matter now, but I'd prefer you not tell Joyce. Basically, when we were young we were attacked by an older boy, another dryad. He'd bullied Reggie for years, made his life miserable, and that day I guess we'd just had enough. We fought him off, but in the scuffle he fell down the stairs. He landed badly and died instantly. We were young, and we freaked out. Rather than calling the Connection, we buried him in a tree. Reggie was the one that pushed him down the stairs and disposed of the body, and he never got over it. He couldn't bear the thought of his children or Joyce finding out he was a killer. He'd have done anything to keep it quiet.' *True.*

'Thank you for telling us. It helps to know a little more about Reggie's character.'

Ronan nodded. 'He was a good man, and that was just a terrible accident. Now, if that's all, I've got things to do.' His eyes lingered on Gato and I didn't like the covetous light in them. Nor did Gato.

'Sure,' I said lightly. 'We'll get out of your hair.'

Safe once again in the confines of Emory's car, I rang Joyce. I got straight to it. 'Did you tell Ronan I was a truth seeker?'

'What? Oh yes. He didn't want me to hire someone so inexperienced, but I explained that you'd stand a better chance than anyone of finding out the truth.'

I bit my lip. 'Okay, thanks. Please don't tell anyone else.'

'I won't tell a soul,' she promised. 'And I'm sure Ronan won't either. He knows about discretion.'

Maybe he did, but I still didn't like the way he'd looked at Gato. 'Fine,' I said aloud. 'Talk to you soon.' I rang off.

Emory raised an eyebrow.

'Most people lie when they talk,' I said. 'The only time Ronan lied was about the rats. That seemed a bit off but I guess he was choosing his words carefully. Anyway, did I tell you Reggie was killed by a griffin? Amber DeLea identified the gouge marks on his body. Do you know any griffins?'

'Griffins are solitary creatures, rarer than dragons. There are probably fewer than thirty in existence. Rumour has it they haven't had a new hatchling in the last century.'

'More immortal creatures?' I sighed.

'Not immortal, just long-lived like the trolls. I know one griffin that will talk to us.' He paused. 'He's a bit of a drunkard, so we might not get much sense out of him.'

'Could he be the killer?' I asked, heart racing at the thought.

Emory shook his head. 'I doubt it. Rumour has it he can barely fly these days, let alone murder someone and disappear. No, I doubt he's the killer but, if a griffin killed Reggie, I expect he'll know who it is. I'll make some enquiries.' He dug out his phone and started to send some emails.

It was time to head out to confront Wokeshire. I pointed the car in the right direction and wasn't surprised when, a few moments later, I picked up some cars tailing us. I spotted Verona in the driving seat of one of them. We had four car loads of the Volderiss cohort with us.

I could feel Nate in my mind. He was travelling in a plane, getting closer all the time, anxious to get back to my side. I tried to reassure him before I drew my awareness away from that spot in my brain.

Wokeshire's residence was similar to Wilf's, but where Wilf's place was well maintained and cared for, Wokeshire's was crumbling and tired. He was in need of some money. I remembered what Emory said about vampyrs killing the dragons and taking their wealth.

'You should stay in the car,' I suggested. 'Taking the prime dragon inside would probably cause some friction.'

'Good.' Emory smiled, though his expression was far from friendly. 'Friction can lead to fire. Let's turn up the heat and see what we get cooking.'

I hesitated. It didn't feel like a good idea to take him. I turned to Gato. 'You'd better stay here,' I said.

Gato barked twice and shook his great head. His eyes met mine and held my gaze.

I sighed and looked away. 'No one is listening to me today,' I bitched. Even so, I let Gato out, and he wasted no time growing into his Battle Cat form. Almost instantly he was the size of a small horse, about the same size as Archie in wolf form. His head was level with mine and his eyes were glowing a sinister red. I leaned forward and gave him a little kiss on his nose. 'Okay,' I agreed. 'I guess you can handle yourself.'

Gato let out a low rumble of agreement, stalked forward and took point. Emory strolled next to me, and the Volderiss vampyrs swarmed around us. Gato used his spiked head to knock loudly on the front door. It splintered and broke. I winced; this wasn't quite the entrance I'd been planning.

Gato stalked into the hall and led us to a reception room. As he burst through the door, I heard hisses from inside.

'Hidey ho!' I called. 'I've got a 4 p.m. appointment with Lord Wokeshire.' I stepped through the ruined doors.

We were in what looked like a tacky throne room. There was a dais at one end with a throne-like chair on it. A handsome older man was sitting on it, looking a little taken a back.

'Sorry about my hound,' I apologised. 'He wasn't with me when I got attacked by your vampyrs the other night, and I think he wants to make up for lost time.'

Gato was vibrating with malevolent energy. If a vampyr tried to take a shot at me, he'd take them down. I suddenly felt like the Volderiss vampyrs were probably overkill; Gato could probably handle this all by himself.

'Rein him in,' Lord Wokeshire ordered.

Head on one side, I considered it. Then I said, 'No, I don't think I will. You tried to kill me. Gato is fine as he is.'

Lord Wokeshire licked his lips, and someone leapt forwards to offer him a goblet of haemoglobin. He took it and drank languidly. I realised that we'd surprised him with our dramatic entrance, and he was trying to regain his equilibrium. Perhaps he'd intended to leave us cooling our heels outside.

Wokeshire looked at Emory with undisguised hatred glittering in his eyes. 'Dragon,' he snarled.

'Vampyr,' Emory sneered back.

I rolled my eyes. 'Well, now we've established our species, let's move on. You ordered an attack on me. Why?' I didn't compel Wokeshire – I didn't think that would be well-received by his clan.

The throne room was bulging with people. Twenty Volderiss vampyrs flanked me, and some thirty to forty Wokeshire clan members were placed strategically across the throne room. They were all dressed in black leather. I guessed they had a dress code.

Lord Wokeshire was staring at me. Suddenly he blinked, and recognition lit his eyes. I frowned at him and raised an eyebrow. What was his deal? He was looking at me like I was Santa Claus, a figment of his imagination made real. He smiled at me. 'I'll discuss it with you. Alone.'

'Me and Gato,' I countered.

Emory glared at me. He didn't want me being anywhere alone with the vampyr but, for all there hostility in the room, I didn't feel like it was directed at me. Most of it was targeting Emory. I didn't like leaving him, but I was confident that he could transform and fly out of trouble if he needed to.

Wokeshire nodded and gestured for me to follow. Gato preceded me, growling sinisterly with every step. He wasn't terribly happy with me for agreeing to this either.

Wokeshire and I went into an adjacent room that was obviously his private office. It was far smaller than the reception room and bookshelves lined every wall. Brown-leather couches faced each other, with a small coffee table in between. I sat on one sofa and Gato stood close to me. He didn't sit; he was poised to attack for me. I really appreciated the sentiment, though I didn't think it was necessary. Weirdly, I wasn't getting any hostility from Wokeshire – in fact, my gut said he was feeling rather hopeful.

He was studying me again, like he was debating what to say. Finally he spoke abruptly. 'A promise is a promise. You need to save my daughter, Mererid.'

I opened my mouth to protest that I hadn't made any promises yet, but he held up a hand and forestalled me.

'Let me explain. My daughter is addicted to Boost. She started taking it about two months ago. A few days ago, she was told her supply would be cut off unless I attacked you. I was reluctant to do so because I am in the middle of negotiations with Volderiss, and I am aware you are under his protection. That is quite evident from the cohort in the other room.'

He frowned and continued. 'But my daughter comes first. Boost is deadly in two ways, firstly if you take the wrong amount and secondly if you stop taking it once you're addicted. If I want my daughter to live then the suppliers are calling the shots. They have ordered me to cut ties with Volderiss.'

He was clearly unhappy about the situation. 'I am head of the clan, as I have been for nearly two centuries. I am not some newly-turned fang. To be subject to another's orders like this – it is untenable! But I am under oath not to work against them or they will withhold Boost from my daughter.'

As Wokeshire watched me, his face carefully blank, I dug out my phone and dialled Nate's number. 'Hey,' I greeted him. 'You've taken lots of drugs, right?'

'Hello to you too, Jinx,' Nate said drily. 'You're with Wokeshire now?'

'Yes,' I confirmed impatiently. 'So you've taken lots of drugs?' I asked again.

'All of them,' Nate admitted. 'It was part of my university rock-and-roll persona.'

'Were you addicted?'

There was a long pause. 'Yes,' he finally confessed. From his tone I could tell he didn't want to admit the truth, perhaps even to himself, but he was well aware he couldn't lie to me as we were bonded.

'Are you still addicted?' I enquired.

'No. After I had your blood, the urge – the addiction – went. I suspect your blood is an overriding addiction.'

'Thanks,' I said, smiling. 'Later.'

I hung up. It was as I'd suspected: since I'd bonded with Nate, I hadn't felt him have a single moment of haze, either with drink or drugs. My blood had cured his need for them.

'You can cure her,' Wokeshire said. He sounded certain.

I tucked my phone back into my pocket. 'I think so. I'm pretty sure I can cure her Boost addiction but the downside is she'll be addicted to wizard's blood instead. The withdrawal is brutal, but it won't kill her.'

Wokeshire weighed the options but I knew he was already on board. It was the only choice that would let him be his own man again and guarantee his daughter's safety. 'Follow me,' he ordered.

I followed him into the kitchens and down into what should have been a wine cellar. It had been converted into a jail. One of the cells was occupied by a female vampyr.

She was fair, whereas Wokeshire was dark; if they were related by blood, I couldn't see the similarity. She was rocking back and forth, her eyes unfocused and unseeing. Gato let out a low growl of warning.

'She's due another hit of Boost,' Wokeshire explained. 'But they are withholding it until you're dead after today's appointment.' *True.*

I didn't really want to go in that cell with a jonesing vampyr. I opened my bum bag and pulled out the little baggie of pink Boost. The female vampyr followed my movements like a lion watching a gazelle. Yeah, I definitely didn't want to go in there until she was high as a kite. I passed the baggie to Wokeshire.

'Either way, this gives you a reprieve. Give her a bump now, then I'll go in. Make sure she doesn't drain me dry.'

'I won't let her kill you,' he promised. That it rang true was the only reason I didn't take to my heels.

Wokeshire put a small line of Boost on a compact mirror and held it out to his daughter through the bars. 'Come, Mererid,' he called.

She leapt from one side of the cell to the other. Instantly she was on the mirror, sniffing up the substance. It took a moment or two to take effect, then she slowly slid down to the floor, her eyes filled with ecstasy, her face slack with pleasure.

Now or never, Jinx.

I gestured to Wokeshire, and he unlocked the cell. I turned to Gato. 'Stay,' I instructed. He sat, but followed my movements with unhappy eyes. As I walked into the cell and Wokeshire closed it behind me, Gato let out a plaintive whine.

Mererid tracked my movements, but her motions were sluggish now. I had to act now before the bump in her power came. I held my wrist out to her as an offering, and she took it. She met my eyes and tried to hypnotise me to make it pleasurable.

'Just bite,' I ordered, avoiding her gaze.

She bit down without further encouragement. Damn, that hurt. I tried not to wince as she pulled at my wrist, sucking and swallowing, lapping at me. It was an alien feeling, and not in a good way.

'Enough,' Wokeshire called.

Drugged higher than the sky on Boost and wizard's blood, Mererid obeyed and dropped my wrist. She slumped back, her eyes rolling in her head. She was out. Only time would tell if I'd helped her or made things a helluva lot worse.

CHAPTER 20

THE CELL DOOR clanged shut behind me as I left. I felt bad for Mererid. If my blood affected hers as it had Nate's, next would come the animalistic rage and strength, followed by super-healing powers, which hopefully would clear the other addiction out of her system. Hopefully. After that she would be in the downswing of an agonising withdrawal that would last days, a week even. Mererid was about to get on a rollercoaster, and I doubted she'd thank me putting her on it.

Wokeshire was watching his offspring with anxious eyes. She might not be the daughter of his blood, but he loved her.

'She'll be okay,' I reassured him. 'It'll be a bumpy ride, but my gut says she'll be fine.'

Wokeshire nodded; I could tell that he believed me, but he was still a cynic. 'If she survives until the morning with no sign of Boost addiction, I'll call you with some further information. If she dies, I'll hunt you until you die too.' *True.*

Gato growled at that and stepped forwards, glaring at the vampyr leader. He didn't like me being threatened; I wasn't much of a fan of it either.

'Noted,' I said. At least he was giving me fair warning.

Wokeshire frowned at my wrist. 'The boost is affecting her healing abilities. Normally her saliva would close your wounds.' He reached out to pick up my wrist, and Gato growled aggressively.

'I'm going to help her,' Wokeshire explained to Gato as he slowly reached out again. Gato allowed him to turn over my wrist. I winced at the sight of it: it was a mess, still oozing thick, sluggish blood, and it would surely leave a scar. I was going to feel lightheaded soon. I'd given blood a few times – to the NHS, not to vampyrs – and I always got a bit dizzy afterwards. This time, I'd given far more than a pint or two.

'If I may?' Wokeshire asked.

I nodded, not quite sure what he was asking. That probably showed how fuzzy my head was. He leaned over my wrist, held it tightly and carefully spit into it. I automatically tried to pull away, but he held on. 'Just a moment,' he cautioned. He carefully smeared his spit into the open wound. Eww. I knew vampyr spittle healed, but there was still something telling me it was unsanitary to let someone dribble into me.

As I watched, the flesh knitted together. Another spit from Wokeshire and the scabs faded away leaving unmarked skin. It was a little sore, but there were no marks to be seen. 'Thank you,' I muttered. I took a step forwards and swayed. He offered me his arm. The world was spinning a little, so I took it.

'She didn't take that much,' he commented.

'I always get dizzy donating blood,' I admitted. 'I guess it just likes staying inside me.'

We took it slowly as we made our way back to the throne room. Gato was dancing apprehensively by my side. As Wokeshire opened the door, the tension was heavy in the air. The two vampyr factions were facing off with Emory in the middle.

I sighed. 'We leave them alone for five minutes,' I said to Wokeshire.

A hint of amusement crept into his eyes, but he remained silent. He had that stoic vampyr vibe nailed.

'Okay,' I said lightly. 'Call me tomorrow when you've decided not to kill me.'

Wokeshire walked me back to Emory. 'Support her,' he instructed. 'She's lightheaded.'

Emory's eyes narrowed dangerously. 'You fed from her,' he said accusingly.

'Not him,' I clarified. 'And it was my suggestion. We've got what we came for.' Kind of. 'Let's go.'

I was feeling all kinds of dizzy, and I wouldn't be able to drive. We'd have to borrow a vampyr from Verona's detail to chauffeur.

I didn't bother to climb in the front seat of the Merc, just slid into the back. Wokeshire leaned over me and clicked on my seatbelt then passed me two cookies and a diet Coke. 'I like full-fat Coke,' I objected. 'I don't like diet anything.'

Wokeshire smiled fractionally. 'I'll get full fat for next time.'

'There won't be a next time,' Emory snarled, getting in the back with me after he had settled Gato. Wokeshire bared his fangs in response.

Verona climbed into the front. Wokeshire shut my door and stood in the waning light, watching our motorcade leave. I waved and he inclined his head. I kinda liked him.

'I like him,' I said.

'He ordered your death,' Emory pointed out.

'Sure, but that wasn't personal. Besides, he's rescinded the order for now.'

'And the "for now" doesn't bother you?' Emory queried.

'Let's not borrow trouble. We've got enough already without asking for more.' I ended the conversation by determinedly munching my way through my cookies and slurping at my diet Coke.

By the time we pulled up to Lucy's, I was feeling a bit better. The world was still moving but at a much more normal rate. Nevertheless, I didn't protest when Emory opened my door, helped me out and offered me his arm.

Gato was walking around me, leaning into my legs. 'I'm okay,' I told him. On the journey he'd settled back to dog size and his eyes were warm caramel. I gave him a stroke. 'Thanks for having my back,' I told him. He barked and licked my hand.

I turned to Verona. 'Wokeshire has rescinded the kill order. You guys can rest. I'll ring tomorrow to tell you if it's back on.'

'Fingers crossed,' she said dryly.

I gave her a fake smile; we both knew she was hoping the order was on rather than off. Bitch.

I leaned on Emory as we walked to the front door. It swung open before we could knock. Lucy was there and she looked rough.

'Woah!' I commented. 'What happened to you?'

She looked exhausted and she had big bags under her eyes. A large yawn split her face. 'Oh, nothing.' She waved away my concern. 'James and I just spent most of the night … erm, you know, so I didn't get much sleep. Come on in.' She watched my slow progress, 'Anyway, you're one to talk! Why are you leaning on Emory like you can't walk? Are you okay?'

'I donated blood,' I explained.

Lucy nodded like that made sense. She's been with me a time or two when I've done it before. 'I made dinner earlier. I've already eaten – I wasn't sure what time you'd be in.'

'Sorry, Luce,' I apologised, sitting down on the sofa.

She smiled. 'It's fine. It's not like I didn't know you keep odd hours when I said you could stay.' She yawned again. 'I'm sorry to flake out, guys, but I'm going to bed. I'm flat out.'

I looked at the clock: it wasn't even 7 p.m. That wasn't like her at all. Lucy is a night owl and an early bird, one of those crazy creatures that can burn both ends of the candle. 'Sleep well.'

She patted Gato as she passed him. He looked at me and let out a soft whine. 'Yeah,' I agreed. 'Go with her.' He padded after her.

Emory squeezed me gently before he settled me safely on the sofa. 'I'll go warm us some food. Will Lucy mind if we eat in here?'

I shook my head. 'Nah. We often eat in the lounge.'

Shortly afterwards, he came back with cottage pie and fresh vegetables. His plate was heaped high, mine only slightly less so. I laughed. 'Emory, I won't be able to eat all that!'

As we ate, we watched the Common news. 'Is there an Other news channel?' I asked curiously.

Emory shook his head. 'No. There aren't any Other TV shows because we haven't worked out how to stop the Common receiving them too. TV is science, not magic.'

'It feels like magic to me,' I countered. 'I love a good movie.'

As I'd expected, I couldn't finish my dinner. Emory ate my leftovers, which felt strangely intimate though I suspect it was really just indicative of the volume of food he needed to eat in a day.

I took up a bowl of food for Gato, crept into Lucy's room and set it down. He climbed carefully off her bed and ate it. When he was done, he went into the bathroom and used her toilet. He flushed, then climbed back onto the bed. He settled his head onto Lucy's tummy, and her hand automatically came to rest on his head.

'Night, pup,' I whispered into the darkness, picking up the bowl and carrying it back downstairs.

'How is she?' Emory asked.

'Okay,' I replied. 'She's sleeping.'

'You're worried,' he stated flatly.

'This isn't like her. Maybe she's coming down with something. Normally she's awake until 1a.m. and up again at 6. She's not someone who sleeps a lot – she says it's a waste of her life.'

Emory made a noncommittal noise and changed the subject. 'I got a call when you were up there. We're meeting our griffin tomorrow at midday. Is that all right?'

I nodded. I had no plans for the following day other than hoping to hear from Wokeshire that Mererid was fully recovered from boost addiction – even if she was battling wizard addiction.

'Are you feeling better?' Emory asked.

'Yes, I'm fine now, thanks.'

'Good. Now tell me what the hell happened.'

Abruptly I realised he had been biting his tongue this whole while, wondering what had gone on. I explained briefly about my discussions with Wokeshire.

'So you're hoping tomorrow he'll call us with the identity of the cartel?'

I shrugged. 'That's the dream.'

'Bit of a long shot.'

'And tracking down a griffin assassin is what?'

'Foolhardy,' he admitted.

'I'm glad we're on the same page at least.'

Emory flashed me a grin. 'Come and sit here, so we can be on the same sofa.'

I moved over and sat next to him. 'You still haven't told me about the brethren,' I commented.

He put a casual arm around my shoulders. 'No, I haven't.' He changed channels on the TV. 'Action movie?'

'Sounds good,' I agreed. Suddenly my day was looking up. So I'd lost a fair amount of blood by letting a vampyr bite me, but at least I was now snuggling on the sofa with a sexy dragon. There were worse ways to spend the evening.

CHAPTER 21

I WOKE ALONE and was disorientated for a moment. Usually Gato was beside me and I looked around for him before remembering that he was with Lucy. I checked the time. 8 a.m. Lucy would be long gone to work. I used the Jack-and-Jill bathroom to brush my teeth and shower.

I went into Lucy's room, and sure enough, she'd already left. Gato was still sleeping on her bed. I frowned. That wasn't like him. 'Hey, pup,' I called softly, stroking his head.

His eyes opened slowly; they were heavy and tired. He let out a soft whine. I kissed him. 'You not feeling well, pup?' He settled his head back down.

'Okay.' I let him go back to sleep. I'd check on him later and bring him some breakfast. I wondered if Lucy's thing was catching. Maybe I shouldn't have let Gato spend the night with her... Who knew how human bugs could affect hell hounds?

I walked into the kitchen diner and stopped abruptly. The table was covered in pastries. At the top of the table, sitting with a coffee and a newspaper, was Emory. Today he was dressed in corporate finest: black suit, black tie, black blazer.

'What's with all the black?' I asked impertinently. 'Everyone in the Other wears black. You, the vampyrs, the brethren. Would some blue kill you?'

Emory smiled. 'Good morning, Jinx. Black hides the bloodstains.' *True.*

'Yeesh.' It was too early for that. I eyed the food. 'Did you make this or go out to a bakery?'

'You sorted breakfast yesterday, so it seemed fair I sort it out today. I called the brethren for breakfast and clothes. I expect they went to a bakery. I wasn't sure what you liked, so I asked for a selection.'

There were *pains au chocolat*, croissants, Danish pastries, jam tartlets, chocolate twists, apricot slices, custard slices – the works. Yum. I poured myself a tea from the pot and doctored it to my taste – milky.

I picked an apricot slice first, reasoning that it contained fruit, so it was virtually healthy. Then I ate a custard slice. Screw it. I reached for a *pain au chocolat*. The pastry was melt-in-your-mouth divine. Gato would love one.

'Gato's not himself,' I commented.

Emory stilled and looked up from the paper. 'He spent the night with Lucy?'

I nodded. Emory folded the paper and got out his

phone. 'Let me make some enquiries.'

'About Gato?'

'I've seen something like this before. Let me confirm it before we worry over something that might be nothing.'

'I shouldn't, like, take him to an Other vet?'

Emory smiled. 'He's a hell hound, he's virtually inde-structible. He'll be fine. Just let him rest. And I'll do some digging.' *All true.* That reassured me a little. He sent a few messages and turned his attention back to me. 'You're looking brighter this morning. Any lingering dizziness?'

I rolled my eyes. 'No, Dad.'

'I assure you, none of my feelings for you are pater-nal.' He sent me a heated glance, which brought the colour to my cheeks. He grinned. 'You blush easily. It's fun.'

'You need to get a hobby,' I commented.

He winked at me and the colour rose again. Dammit. 'Our meeting is midday, right?' I asked.

Emory nodded. 'Yes, but it's in London so we need to factor in travel time.'

Although we were in what you'd call Greater London, we'd need to take a train into London proper. No point driving a car with traffic, congestion charges and parking rates. 'Train?' I suggested.

Emory wrinkled his nose in distaste. 'I'll sort the transport.'

We had a lazy morning before getting ready to leave. Gato had perked up a little, but I decided to leave him at Lucy's until he was feeling better. He ate breakfast with gusto, which I found encouraging, but then he slunk back upstairs to sleep again. I cast a worried glance after him.

'He'll be fine,' Emory reassured me. *True.*

I smiled back and let myself believe him. If anything happened to Gato or Lucy, I'm pretty sure my world would implode.

I copied Emory and changed into smart clothes: suit trousers and a black blouse. I reluctantly threw on a suit jacket too. My leather jacket had wolf teeth marks, probably not the best look if we were going for business-like. I checked my pockets carefully. All empty. I double-checked that Glimmer was still on the bedside table. Taking such a big dagger into London was asking for trouble.

I kissed Gato goodbye and texted Lucy to let her know he was still at her house as he wasn't feeling well. I'd left him dinner, so she didn't need to hurry home for him – after all, he could use the toilet and flush it afterwards. I didn't tell her that part in case she thought I was crazy.

I grabbed a large black bag and stuffed my parents', Miller's and Evergreen's files inside it then followed Emory out of the house. It was novel to not have a procession of vampyrs following me, and it made me feel less like I was part of a travelling carnival. Emory offered me his arm. I felt absolutely fine but I took it anyway because I could. And he smelled nice.

We were in Chalfont St Giles. I had no idea how Emory knew where we were going but he led us easily to the village green. It was 11 a.m. as we approached a park bench, and I looked around to see where his transport was. I couldn't see any fancy cars.

'It'll just be a minute,' Emory promised. 'I said 11.05.'

He was right. My jaw dropped as a black Bell 206L-3 LongRanger helicopter flew into sight and landed expertly on the green at precisely 11.05. In my skydiving days, I'd watched with envy when a few friends had jumped out of a helicopter. Unfortunately the weather had turned before it was my turn, and the helicopter was grounded. I had never used one commercially either, so this was a real thrill.

Emory tugged me forwards to it, just in case I had any doubts that this was our transport. I ducked down automatically as we moved under its rotating blades then he helped me into a cream leather seat. Once I was buckled in, he shut the door and buckled up as well.

He passed me a headset so we could talk. 'Good to go. London Heliport.'

'Roger, Prime Elite,' came the response from the pilot. The helicopter set off so smoothly that I barely registered that we were flying.

'Gato will be gutted he missed this,' I said.

Emory smiled. 'He can come next time.' He looked very relaxed.

'You really do like flying,' I commented.

'I love it.'

'Me too, though it's weird to be in a helicopter and know I'm not going to jump out of it.'

Emory gave me a startled look. 'What?'

'I used to skydive,' I explained.

He grinned. 'Of course you'd be a skydiver.' He shook his head.

'You think I'm nuts?'

He met my eyes. 'I think you're perfect.' *True.*

I was blushing again. I'm a lot of things, but perfect isn't one of them. I sent him a shy smile and then distracted myself by looking at the tiny buildings and fields that we were passing over. The winter sky was clear and crisp, and we could see for miles.

The helicopter was flying at speed – we'd be in London far too soon for my liking. This bad boy could fly for nearly three hours, and we'd probably be there in less than twenty minutes. Shame.

I was right. We landed all too soon. 'Stay on standby,' Emory instructed the pilot.

'Roger,' the pilot confirmed. I gave him a thumbs up, and he returned the gesture. He was young, and he looked as excited to be flying the helicopter as I had been riding in it.

Emory and I left the heliport and moved quickly towards a chauffeur-driven Bentley Mulsanne. Of course, what else would it be? 'You live in a different world,' I said to Emory.

He laughed. 'So do you.'

I gave a wry smile. He wasn't wrong, but that wasn't what I'd meant.

He held the door open for me and I climbed in with all the elegance and poise of a drunken gazelle. The interior of the car didn't disappoint; it was all luxury leather and free bottled water. How the other half live.

Emory was frowning, tapping away at his phone.

'Problem?' I asked.

'Politics. Some issues in-house.'

'Dragon issues?'

'Dragon issues.'

I didn't pry; he'd tell me if he wanted me to know. And he was bankrolling my best luxury-vehicle day ever, so I wasn't going to annoy him right now.

The Bentley came to a stop outside London Stock in the Ram Quarter. It was still only 11.30 a.m. and according to the notice outside, the restaurant didn't open until noon but that apparently didn't stop clients like Emory walking in early. He was greeted by the maître d' as 'Mr Elite', and we were shown to an exclusive room which was already occupied.

'The tasting menu for all of us,' Emory ordered. 'And some privacy.'

The maître d' nodded, withdrew and closed the door. We were left with a man who appeared to be completely sozzled. He was dressed in a suit that was so rumpled and worn, he looked like he'd slept in it. His hair was shoulder length, mousy and lank and I doubted it had been brushed in weeks. Despite that, he didn't smell and was clearly clean, if unkempt. His eyes were a striking brown, flecked with gold and yellow.

'Shirdal,' Emory greeted him.

'Dragon Prime Elite,' Shirdal slurred. 'I'd bow, but I think I'd fall over.'

Emory grimaced. 'Are you still drunk from last night, or have you been working on it this morning?'

'Ah, this, my fine Azhdar, is the result of weeks of hard drinking. I am a consummate professional. I haven't been sober for over a month,' he stated with a great deal of pride. He spoke with a faint accent, but I couldn't place it.

Something about his attitude rubbed me up the wrong way. Alcoholism is an addiction and a path to destruction, not a jolly old hobby. 'You're drunk,' I accused.

'Constantly, my dear,' Shirdal replied. 'It's how one lives with one's actions after centuries of disrepute.'

'Any recent actions of disrepute?' Emory enquired lightly.

'Not for nine years and 203 days. But who's counting?'

'What counts as disrepute?' I asked curiously.

'Torture, death and maiming,' Shirdal slurred. 'It turns out my species are extraordinarily good at it. I, however, am a failure, a griffin with a conscience. I am an absurdity! An outcast!' He was going full dramatic, making wide gestures, flinging his limbs around. In another life he would have been a thespian. He was growing on me, despite myself.

'Can I show you some pictures?' I asked.

He winked at me. 'Sweetheart, you can show me anything you like.'

I grimaced; great, the drunk griffin was flirting with me. On days like this, I wished Lucy knew about the Other realm. She'd have a giggle with me about the absurdity of life.

'Of course,' Shirdal continued, 'while we may be sexually compatible while I'm in this form, we're not compatible as mates. Unlike dragons, of course, who are compatible with humans.' He lowered his voice like he was going to whisper, but when he spoke he was still pretty loud. 'That's how you get the brethren. They're the offspring that don't become dragon. Fifty percent dragon, fifty percent human. And one hundred percent no fun.'

Emory glared at him. 'If you're quite done hitting on Jinx and giving away our secrets, can we get to the matter at hand?'

Shirdal smiled smarmily at me. 'Can't Jinx be the

matter at my hand?'

'No,' Emory said firmly.

Normally I would have been annoyed that someone had dared to speak on my behalf, but he was right. Big fat no from me, too.

I cleared my throat. 'I have some photos for you to look at. I want you to tell me what you can about the crime scenes.'

There was a knock at the door. 'Enter,' Emory called. A procession of staff came in and laid three place settings and a veritable feast on the table. The food was fancy and fine, not like anything I'd ever eaten before. There were mushroom parfaits, red mullet salad, roast turkey, roast cod, and everything had an Asian twist. My mouth watered, and my tummy growled.

Emory smiled. 'Food first?' he suggested.

'I'm much sharper after food,' Shirdal agreed. He'd have to be; he couldn't get any duller.

We fell on the food. Each plate was small but perfect, and after ten courses I was stuffed. 'That was amazing,' I said.

'Satisfying,' agreed Shirdal with a loud belch.

I wrinkled my nose. Apparently griffins, besides being non-stop killers, were also lacking in manners. My mum would not have approved.

CHAPTER 22

A FTER WE'D EATEN, we waited for the staff to clear the tables before we got down to business. Emory asked for teas and coffees and that we not be disturbed again.

I was about to draw the files out of my bag when my phone rang. Number unknown. I answered, wondering if it was going to be another death threat.

'Jinx. It's Wokeshire.' I hoped it was a good sign that he was calling me, and I put my mobile on speakerphone so Emory could listen in. I wasn't worried about Shirdal; he was so wasted I doubted he'd remember anything he heard.

'How is Mererid?' I asked.

'She's showing no signs of Boost withdrawal. She's experiencing wizard blood withdrawal but is well otherwise, and she has regained her mental faculties. Although she's still in quite a lot of pain, she's asked me to pass along her thanks for freeing her from the Boost cycle.'

'I'm glad to hear that. It would be helpful if she could tell me a little more about her experiences in Boost when she's feeling stronger.'

'I'll pass along what I already know,' Wokeshire said. 'Her dealer was someone she knew only as Dave, and she used to meet him outside the Eden Centre. She knew Boost was a drug manufactured for Others, and she was eager to try a new high. Now she is old, novel experiences are hard to come by.'

He paused then continued. 'It was a mistake. Boost gave her a high unlike any other drug and after that came the surge in power. She was faster than anything I'd ever seen, even by vampyr standards. At first the low after the drug wore off was minor – a bit of drowsiness and lethargy but nothing more. But the more she took, the longer the lethargy continued and she reached the stage where she couldn't move without it. She was all but immobile and her mind was simply not there. She couldn't, or wouldn't, communicate with me or answer any questions.

'I tracked down her dealer at the Eden Centre and I was told that she needed more Boost to survive now that she was an addict. Without her next bump, she'd stop moving and eventually she would die.'

He cleared his throat. 'The dealer told me that they wouldn't supply her or any of the Wokeshire vampyrs unless I helped them. First, they wanted me to kill you, then help them obtain a further supply of unicorn horn. Apparently there was an issue recently with their herd.

'I was given an invitation to a masked ball that is taking place tonight – I've arranged for it to be sent to you. It's supposedly a charity ball, but its main purpose is for the cartel to secure additional funding and access more unicorn herds. I did some digging and had a chat with Dave. The ball is being held at the head of the cartel's home. Security will be tight, but the whole thing will be off the Connection's radar.'

'Is Dave still alive?' I enquired. I wasn't too hopeful that bobble-hat Dave had a bright future.

'For now. I didn't want his employers to suspect anything, so he was roughed up, and his mind was cleared,' Wokeshire replied grimly.

I winced. Poor Dave's mind was going to have more holes in it than Swiss cheese.

Wokeshire continued his rundown on Boost. 'For most drug takers, Boost gives them a bump in their power. It's become incredibly popular among the young, but very few get addicted as Mererid did, and fewer still have died. The cartel want to ramp up production to meet the rising demand, but they're struggling to acquire the volume of unicorn horn they require. Some of the very rich have unicorns on their estate for security purposes. The leader of the cartel is going to ask that those at the ball give up their herds for Boost production. In return, they'll receive a cut of the profits. Unicorns are heavily regulated, and getting more through other channels is proving difficult.'

It gave me a great deal of satisfaction to know that I had ruined the cartel's manufacturing process so significantly by liberating the herd. It was worth getting my calf gouged for.

'So I'm to take your place at the ball tonight?' I clarified.

'Now I'm not under their control, I won't be going,' Wokeshire confirmed.

'They won't like that.'

'I will not cower in the face of some shadowy organisation. I am Lord Wokeshire, not some new fang. If they come for me, I will be waiting.' With that, he hung up.

I tucked away my phone.

'I like charity balls,' commented Emory.

'I'm glad one of us does.' I sighed, mentally cataloguing the clothes I'd brought with me. Absolutely no dresses. Lucy might have something I could borrow, but her skin tone was paler than pale and her hair was bright blonde so we weren't exactly on the same colour palette. Ah well, beggars couldn't be choosers; there would be something that would fit me at least. Lucy loved dresses; she'd have everything from wedding attire to cocktail dresses, and hopefully a full-length ball gown.

'I like balls,' Shirdal murmured. 'I cut a fine figure on the dance floor.'

I grimaced as I imagined him staggering around a

dance floor. 'I think we'll be okay. This is a stealth operation. Less is more.'

'I am affronted.' He wagged a finger in my direction and sat upright. 'I am the soul of stealth and discretion, I assure you. I am a griffin of the finest order.' It was hard to imagine this human as a griffin, and I certainly wasn't working up any fear. I knew griffins had deadly talons, but while he was in the Common, he was as much a threat as any other drunken bum.

'Let's get back to business,' Emory said to him. 'The ball isn't your concern.'

I pulled the files out of my bag and handed over Miller's first. To my surprise, Shirdal took it with steady hands and started reading quickly. His eyes were narrowed intently; gone were all traces of the drunken lout who'd been there moments before. Huh.

'An organised kill, for sure. This is no accident. I'd suggest you're looking for a dryad killer. Next file.'

I passed him Reggie's. Shirdal looked through it carefully, his golden-yellow eyes moving incredibly fast. 'Griffin,' he confirmed. 'Definitely griffin. This has no finesse, so I'd say it's the work of one of the younger assassins – Charlize or Fergal. But the more salient question is who hired them?'

He passed back the file and I dug out the final one. My tummy was churning with nerves. I wanted a lead for my parents' death – I *needed* one. I'd been searching for so long.

He opened it, paused, then looked at me. 'Ah,' he said softly, 'no wonder you looked familiar. You're Mary and George's daughter.'

'You knew them?'

He nodded. 'Yes. They were quite insistent about holding griffins responsible for their actions, and I met with them on a number of occasions. They arrested me once. I wondered what had become of them when they disappeared so abruptly. You were only a baby at the time, I believe.' *True.* There was sadness in his eyes. 'It seems whatever they were running from caught up with them.'

'Who?' I asked intently. 'Who killed them?'

'An assassin of the highest order. This is the work of our most expensive asset – Bastion.' *True.*

Emory grimaced.

But I had a name; I had a name and a lead. Finally. 'Thank you.'

Shirdal shook his head. 'Don't thank me. If you go looking for Bastion, you'll die.' *True.* 'I'm a nice griffin, but Bastion is not. He was hired to kill them. Look to his employer, not to him.'

It was probably good advice, but I'd had seven years of searching for the bastard who was responsible for my parents' deaths, and it was this Bastion. He may have had orders, but he was the one that had sliced and diced them like so much flesh at a meat market.

'How do you go about hiring a griffin?' I asked.

'*You* don't,' Shirdal said firmly. 'Let Prime Elite find out. He might survive making enquiries.'

I opened my mouth to argue but Emory touched me on the shoulder and shook his head. 'We haven't got a lot of time,' he reminded me. 'We need to get ready for the ball, which includes getting to the location with plenty of time to recce it. We're done here.'

For now, I thought rebelliously. 'I just need the bathroom.'

Once there, I freshened up, then slid out my phone and texted Mo: *Need you to dig into something sensitive. A professional assassin known as Bastion. See what you can find.*

Almost immediately I got a beep back. *On it.* Maybe Mo wouldn't find anything, but if this guy was such a big deal then he'd have made splashes in both realms. Interpol, MI5, MI6, the FBI – one of the alphabets would have something on him. And if they did, Mo would find it.

I slid the phone back into my pocket with a satisfied smirk. There were some things I was happy to let Emory take the lead on, but this wasn't one of them. I'd waited seven years to get this far. Ready or not, Bastion, I was coming for you.

CHAPTER 23

EMORY SETTLED THE bill. By the time we walked out of the restaurant, the car was waiting for us. We settled in and headed back to the heliport. 'Do you want to talk about it?' he asked. 'Your parents?'

I shook my head. 'Not now. We need to focus on Reggie and Conrad and getting justice for them. Tonight we infiltrate the masked ball, see if we can break into the head of the cartel's home and get the information we need to bring them all down.'

Sure. It seemed so simple when you rattled it off like that. Jeez, we were nuts.

'We can notify the Connection,' Emory continued.

I rolled my eyes. We *could* notify the Connection – but there was zero way Emory was going to notify them. His working relationship with them was so cool it bordered on glacial. No, he was just trying to persuade me that's what he would do; in truth, he would go off alone without me.

'Nice try,' I commented drily.

Emory grinned. 'Worth a go.'

We arrived at the heliport and made our way back to our chopper. The young pilot gave us an enthusiastic wave. We climbed in, and he started the blades spinning.

This time, my mind wasn't on the journey. It wasn't on the ball either. I was remembering finding my parents' bodies. There had been blood everywhere. They were so badly mutilated that it was difficult to accept it was them, that they were really gone. It had taken a lot of therapy to get my head around it.

Death changes a body; the heartbeat, the movement of the chest, whatever it is that makes us *alive* is gone. And what is left behind is just blood and sinew and bone.

Vampyrs might not eat food but their chests still rise and fall like they were breathing. I don't know whether it's an affectation or a genuine need, but even if they are undead there is still something about them that says *life*.

Emory nudged my knee with his. 'You okay?' There was concern in his green eyes.

'It brings it all back,' I admitted. 'But I'm fine.' *Lie.* I looked down from the window and stared unseeing at the tiny houses that had so delighted me earlier.

I looked back at Emory as he threaded his fingers with mine. His touch steadied me, and I felt his calmness washing over me. There wasn't a hint of pity in his emotions. He was busy on his phone, tapping messages one handed, the modern dragon on the go. He squeezed my hand, and I dropped my gaze back to the window. I didn't pull away, though. Emory left me to my thoughts, and I let them fester.

By the time we landed, I'd given myself a firm talking to. *Buck up, Jinx, this is a bumpy ride, and you need to keep going.* Emory helped me out of the helicopter and kept our hands laced together as we walked back to Lucy's. I tried to tell myself that the butterflies in my stomach were indigestion.

It was 3 p.m. and Lucy was still at work. 'Gato?' I called upstairs. There was a bump from above us, and a moment later he thundered down the stairs. He was wagging his tail, looking happy and full of energy.

'Hey, pup,' I greeted him, kissing the top of his head when he was level with me. 'I was worried about you.' Something in me eased now that I could see Gato had recovered from whatever was ailing him.

Emory passed me the cream card that had been posted through the door. The invitation said: *Lord and Lady Wokeshire are invited to attend a masked ball.* Emory and I would probably be able to get in with no problem, assuming our masks were big enough and the doormen had never met Lord and Lady Wokeshire. It was a gamble we'd have to take.

The address was Rithean Castle in Wales, about an hour from my Liverpool address. It would take us at least four hours to drive there. Using the helicopter wouldn't help us make a discreet entrance if we were trying to stay under the radar.

I'd been to Rithean Castle exactly once. Three weeks earlier Hester and I had been given a voucher for a day's spa treatment there, courtesy of a grateful client. There were two giant hot tubs to relax in, and I'd had a lovely thermal mud-wrap. If I'd known I was in the home of a criminal mastermind, it would have been less relaxing. But the visit was useful – at least I had some idea of how to find my way around.

'It starts at 8p.m. We'll have to leave soon if we want to make it. The helicopter wouldn't be too subtle,' I pointed out.

'Helicopter is the easiest way to travel round London,' Emory said.

I grinned. 'Some would say the tube is easier.'

Emory waved that away. 'As a dragon, I'm not a fan of the underground, we prefer to see the sky.'

'You could always fly us there,' I joked. 'I could ride on your back.'

Emory's eyes darkened. 'Only a dragon's mate is allowed to ride on his or her back.'

I reddened. 'Sorry, I didn't know.' Open mouth, insert foot.

'No problem.' He said it lightly, but I still felt a little embarrassed. I remembered Joyce once telling me talking about someone's magic use in the Common like asking about their dick size. From Emory's expression, asking to ride him was a similar faux pas.

He took mercy on me and changed the subject. 'I took the liberty of getting you a dress delivered for the ball because I assumed you wouldn't have one here. I'll call someone to sort out the masks – I'm assuming you don't have two masks floating about?'

I blinked. 'No, I don't.'

'They're on your bed.'

'They?'

'The dresses. Over the years, I've learnt that women like to have a choice.'

'And do said women also like having their locks being picked?'

Emory grinned unrepentantly. 'The Brethren have many skills.'

He'd bought me multiple dresses? I'm not often a girly-girl, but even I was a little excited to see what options I'd been gifted. In his human form Emory positively dripped style, so I couldn't imagine he'd got me something awful. I could overlook a little breaking-and-entering if it got me some beautiful dresses, though Lucy might not agree with me.

I dashed upstairs, mentally cataloguing what shoes or bags I could make do with. On my bed were three huge dress boxes. I took off the first lid and just managed to supress a squeal of delight. The dress was a rich emerald green. My first thought was that it would match Emory's eyes perfectly, but I clamped down hard on that. It was silk, a spaghetti-strap, V-necked dress with a full skirt that flowed to the ground. It had a slit up one side and a pocket on the other. Yes! No matter what the other options were, this was a winner because it had pockets!

Nestled in the box was a matching clutch bag. I picked up the dress, held it up against me and was a hundred percent sold on it, but then I set it aside and dutifully looked in the other two boxes.

The next dress was blue and matched *my* eyes perfectly. It was an A-line, floor-length tulle dress overlaid with small sections of lace and sequins. It was stunning – but no pockets. If I hadn't seen the green one already, I'd have fallen in love with the blue one. There was also a lace and beaded blue clutch in the box.

The last box contained a maroon dress with a beautiful full skirt and a princess neckline. It was gorgeous, and there was a matching bag. No pockets.

All three, with their bright jewel colours, were perfect for my skin tone. Whoever had picked them had an eye for colour. But I was going to wear the green one. I'd have to go braless but it looked like it had a good amount of built-in support.

I was about to try it on when Emory called up, 'The car will be here in half an hour.'

'Half an hour?' I yelled in panic. I couldn't be ready in half an hour! 'Can you feed Gato dinner?' I shouted down. Yes, Emory was the dragons' Prime Elite, but I needed every minute to get ready. He'd just have to do the chores.

I texted Lucy, explained I was going out of town and asking if she could look after Gato for me. She quickly agreed. Lucy is the best.

I used her hot brush to give my normally straight hair a little more body and swept on makeup in record time, then I stepped into the green dress. To my relief, it fit me perfectly. On the floor next to the door were three brand-new shoe boxes. I opened them: sure enough they each held a pair of shoes to match each of the dresses. I selected the green heels and stepped into them, thankful they weren't open toed, and my chipped nail varnish wouldn't show.

'Car is here,' Emory called up.

'Just one minute,' I promised. I spritzed on my favourite Chanel and twisted the top half of my hair up in a neat chignon, leaving the bottom layer to tumble down onto my shoulders. I secured it with bobby pins, and I was good to go. My one minute had turned into five, but I still didn't think that was bad going.

I headed down the stairs. Emory was waiting at the bottom wearing a new suit. It was black, of course, but now he had on a green shirt that matched my dress perfectly. He looked edible. I paused a moment too long on the top step, staring at him.

'You went green too,' I commented to distract him from my gawping. He watched me as I continued down the stairs, his eyes dark and his expression unreadable. My mouth went dry. 'You look great,' I babbled.

Emory's eyes swept me from head to toe. 'You're beautiful, Jessica.' His voice was low and seductive, and a thrill shot through me as I heard my name on his lips. I wasn't feeling even a little business like.

'Thank you,' I managed. He took a step towards me, forcing me to tilt my head to look up at him. My heart was hammering in my chest. There was no mistaking his intention.

'You can't kiss me,' I blurted out. 'You're my client.'

His eyes warmed. 'Jessica … you're fired.' He leaned down and kissed me and, God help me, I let him.

CHAPTER 24

EMORY WAS A man who knew how to kiss. He took turns being soft and gentle, and then sweeping and possessive. My tummy was full of butterflies, and the bones in my legs had apparently melted. When he pulled back, it took me a few moments to regain my mental faculties. 'That was nice,' I blurted out.

Emory smirked. 'I wasn't aiming for nice.' He leaned back in and kissed me again until my brain started melting out of my ears. 'Nice?' he purred in my ear.

I shook my head, incapable of speech.

He laughed softly. 'Good.' As he tugged my hand and led us to the front door, he said, 'Be a good boy, Gato.'

Outside, a limousine was waiting for us. I blinked at it, 'More room for us,' Emory explained.

I nodded: space between me and Emory seemed like a good idea, especially if I needed my brain to start working anytime soon. But despite all that space, when I climbed in the back seat he sat right next to me. 'Where were we?' he asked. 'Oh yes.' And he kissed me again.

I'd like to say I resisted valiantly, but I didn't. Not

even a little. We had a four-hour journey ahead of us, and necking in the car suddenly seemed like a brilliant use of my time.

Things were getting rather heated, and I was just thinking about the pros and cons of having sex with Emory in a limo when he pulled back. 'We'd better eat,' he said with some reluctance. He gave me one final peck on the lips and moved to the other end of the car where an insulating bag sat next to a beribboned cardboard box.

What? I'd been one minute away from stripping off, and now we were having dinner? It took me a few moments to shift gears, and I felt a little grumpy. It had been an age since I'd had a social orgasm, and it didn't seem fair of Emory to deprive me of it.

He returned to my side carrying two cling-film wrapped bowls of pasta. 'Not ideal,' he said apologetically. 'But it saves time.' He passed me a bowl and a fork, and I took them automatically.

'Jinx. Are you with me?' he asked.

I frowned. 'No, I'm with the "you" of five minutes ago who was a lot more fun,' I groused.

His smile widened. 'I promise you a whole lot more fun, but maybe not in the back of a limo for our first time.'

I rolled my eyes. 'Of course, you would have standards.'

He kissed on my neck. 'So do you,' he pointed out

softly. 'And I'm not letting the passion of the moment override them.'

Well, damn. That was kind of sweet, but I still didn't like him taking the choice away from me. It occurred to me that he had choices too; consent wasn't a one-way street. I told my hormones to settle down from the cha-cha they were doing, took a few deep breaths and centred myself like my parents had taught me.

Feeling calmer, I unwrapped my cling film and dug in. 'Sorry,' I muttered. 'It turns out I get organgry.'

'Organgry?' he repeated, bemused.

'Orgasm angry. You know, like hangry is hungry angry.'

He laughed. 'I'll make a note of that for next time.'

I gave him a hoity-toity stare. 'See that you do.' But, annoyed as I might have been a few moments earlier, I knew he was right. We needed our business heads. This ball wasn't going to be a lark, and we had to be prepared.

'Have you got any idea of the layout of the castle?' I asked. 'I've been there before for a spa day, but I only went into the commercial side of the property.'

'You like spa days?'

'I *love* spa days. Focus, please.'

He pulled out his phone and brought up the floor plan. 'Here's where I think the ball will be, and my sources tell me this is the library. Next to the library is the office.' He frowned. 'Rithean Castle appears to be owned by Karkadun Limited. I've got people on it, but Karkadun is owned by another company called Flight Fallow. So I'm digging into that company too.'

I put down my bowl, pulled out my phone and texted the two names to Mo with a request that he find out the owner of the corporations. He replied immediately saying he was on it and that he hadn't found out anything more about Boost or Bastion.

'I've got Mo looking into it,' I told Emory. 'That name Karkadun rings a bell, though.' I racked my brain. Suddenly the light flicked on. 'Ah! I remember – the same company owns the farm that Dave told me was the centre of the drug operations.'

Emory frowned. 'I should have given you that infor-mation earlier. Sorry, I'm used to flying solo.'

'No problem,' I said. 'I'm the same.'

Emory tucked a stray lock of hair behind my ear. 'We seem to make a good team,' he observed.

'So far so good.'

As we looked at the floor plan of the castle, both of us trying to memorise the layout, my phone lit up again. I reached for it, hoping it was Mo. No such luck: it was Leo Harfen. 'Leo,' I snapped. 'You mind cleared me!'

'Ah.' He paused. 'Did I?'

'Yes!'

'I don't remember doing it. Was it me in the past, the now, or the future?'

I opened my mouth to say 'now, of course' but then closed it. When he'd come to my door, he'd been old – like *really* old. Leo Harfen was an elf who'd dabbled far too much in the Third realm and time was no longer linear for him. He was a muddle of a man, literally lost in time. He was a word of caution for anyone thinking of dabbling too much in time.

'Future,' I admitted grudgingly.

'Ah, well then. I'll make a note in my diary so I remember to do it in the future. Thanks for letting me know. I was just calling because I had a note to do so. This must have been why. Take care Jessica Sharp.' He hung up.

I glared at the phone. Every time I had messed in the Third realm, I had caused what I had been trying to avoid. 'Stupid elf,' I muttered, slipping my phone into the pocket of my dress. The novelty of that pocket wasn't wearing off.

As I dropped the phone in, I felt something other than my lockpick set. Glimmer. I swore darkly and pulled it out. 'What the hell do you think you're doing here?' I shouted at it. 'I left you on my bedroom table.' A passing road light caught the blade, making it – glimmer. It sang a cheerful, chirpy hello into my mind.

'No, not hello,' I groaned. 'I'm mad at you. You better behave. Now shut up and stop singing.' I put it back into my pocket and it fell quiet, but with an injured air.

Emory was watching me, eyes wide. 'Did you just tell Glimmer to shut up?'

'You know about Glimmer?'

'The magical blade that the Harfen elves made, which can make the Common become the Other? Yeah, it's been mentioned a time or two across the centuries. Can I touch it?' he asked reverently.

I shrugged. 'Sure.' I tugged it back out and it burst into joyful song. 'Quit that,' I said firmly. I turned to Emory. 'Do you hear the singing?'

He shook his head. 'No, I imagine that's just for its bonded.'

'Bonded? Really? I'm already bonded to enough things. I don't want any more.' I had Gato, Nate and now Glimmer; it was a miracle there was enough of me to go around.

I passed Emory the blade carefully. He turned it to examine it and swore as it bit into his flesh. 'Glimmer!' I yelled angrily.

'Just a nick.' Emory ruefully passed the blade back to me, lifted his bleeding finger to his mouth and sucked away the blood. 'I should have known better than to touch a bonded weapon.'

Glimmer sang an agreement. 'You're in my bad books,' I told it firmly and put it back in my pocket. 'It's a very badly behaved blade,' I complained. 'It keeps appearing in my pocket when I try to leave it at home.'

'It appears when you have need of it,' Emory explained. 'Don't complain.'

'It doesn't bode well that it's appeared before our ball.'

Emory flashed me a cheeky smirk. 'Don't worry. I have contingency plans.'

The intercom buzzed and we heard the chauffeur's voice. 'Prime, we are ten minutes away.'

'Thank you,' Emory replied. He reached into a compartment in the car and pulled out a large jewellery box. He opened it. 'Here.' His eyes were serious.

I opened the box; inside was a teardrop-shaped emerald pendant. The stone was huge. 'Is that real?' I squawked. 'I can't wear that!'

He grinned. 'Dragon's hoard, remember? You can wear it. It will be safer on your neck than in my pocket.' He unfastened the intricate gold chain and slid it around my neck. The emerald rested heavily on my sternum.

'I'm not really a jewellery girl,' I tried to explain.

Emory shrugged. 'We're at a rich person's ball. We need to fit in.' Fair point.

He opened the fancy cardboard box I'd noticed earlier. In it were two masks decorated with peacock feathers. 'Subtle,' I muttered.

'The obscenely rich don't do subtle, they do vain. We'll fit right in.'

The masks were well made and mine had a hair slide

so I could secure it to my hair. It was close fitting enough to hide my eyes, but I still had a good visual range.

There was a sign for the castle and we turned into the driveway. The private road was guarded by towering stone eagles and mighty balustrades. The drive was lined with trees, planted in uniform distances from one another. Between the trees were lit and flickering torches, casting shadows and smoking in the night. The whole thing was supposed to be atmospheric but all it was doing was making me feel jumpy.

We drew up to the castle. The moon was full and the courtyard was bathed in light. The car stopped at a red carpet and Emory climbed out first then offered me his hand. There was a man in a uniform manning the entrance but he didn't even ask for our invite. I guess rocking peacock feathers was enough. Emory had been right; we didn't attract a second glance. The room was already filling nicely with all manner of fine people. Suddenly Emory let out a low growl.

'What's up?' I asked.

'The man in red by the string quarter, he's a dragon. One of mine.' The man Emory was referring to was wearing a bright red suit and mask. A shade or two pinker and he would have looked like a flamingo.

'Will he recognise you with your mask?'

'Undoubtedly.' Emory picked up two champagne flutes from a passing waiter and turned away.

'What's his name?'

'Fabian.'

'I'll keep my eye on Fabian, and we'll try to keep your back to him,' I said. 'Do you think he's here for the charity ball?'

'No. Fabian has been stirring up some of my in-house issues. If he's here, it's because he's involved.' Emory's expression darkened.

'We're at a ball,' I reminded him. 'Lighten up a little or you'll scare people.' And draw their attention.

'True.' He forced a smile. 'Let's dance.'

We joined the throng of dancers. I did my best not to bat an eyelid as I saw a troll and an elemental walk in. I wondered if Emory and Fabian felt vulnerable being in their human form among all those in the Other. Then I inadvertently made eye contact with a woman across the room. She had the same feel as Amber DeLea – was she a witch? Maybe she was Amber's renegade.

The feel of the room was relaxed and decadent. After we'd done a few more turns on the dance floor, the crowd was really thickening. It was disheartening to see how many people were on Team Bad Guys.

We waited until there was a lull in the music then left the dance floor, ostensibly to find the toilets. Thankfully the halls were empty, and we quickly made our way to the library.

This was a library to rival Lady Sorrell's, Hester's

grandmother. There was a roaring fire, and drinks and canapés were set up on a side table. Uh-oh. We were in the wrong place: this was where the cartel members were coming to discuss things privately. I felt a frisson of fear.

Emory reached the same conclusion and headed back to the door, but before we could reach it in came Dave. He was dressed in a suit and tails but, even with his mask, there was no hiding the fact that his face was black and blue. He looked unhappy.

'Prime Elite. Jinx.' He identified us both with ease. 'I've been told to ask you to come with me. If you're thinking about refusing, we have your hell hound.' *True.*

How the hell did they have Gato? Was Lucy okay? Dread was thrumming through me and I didn't have any thought other than complying. I couldn't risk Gato, or Lucy. I sent a stricken look to Emory and he squeezed my shoulder reassuringly. 'Lead the way,' he said calmly.

Dave pulled out some handcuffs. 'I've got to put these on you.'

Emory looked at me then nodded. He was allowing himself to be cuffed for Gato's sake – and for me.

Dave clicked the cuffs onto Emory and they instantly started to glow blue. 'Magic inhibitors,' Emory explained. 'They stop me changing into dragon form.'

I was similarly cuffed and I felt a surge of panic as the constant presence of my magic fell away. But despite that, I felt an encouraging presence reaching out to me. Nate:

we were still bonded, magic inhibitors or no.

I closed my eyes and did my best to imagine Rithean Castle. I hoped it would be enough for Nate to work out where I was and that I needed rescuing.

'Follow me and your hound won't get hurt,' Dave instructed.

For the first time in my life, I had no buzz of a lie or a truth. If I hadn't been quite so scared, it would have been rather liberating. This is what normal people felt like all the time but, for me, the uncertainty was strange.

Dave had cuffed our wrists behind our backs and reached out to remove our masks. 'Hey!' I protested. 'Careful of the hair!'

He gave me a dark smile. 'Your hair is the least of your concerns, babe.' He seemed a little excited by the prospect. Any kindness I felt towards bobble-hat Dave melted away.

He moved between us and started tugging us through the castle. We crossed the courtyard, where there was no sign of our car. When we reached the other wing of the great building, he pushed Emory in front of him. 'Down here. And no tricks or she'll be the one that gets it.'

Emory nodded calmly, like he was used to being abducted, and walked easily down the narrow steps. I followed behind much more slowly; having my arms behind my back made me nervous about falling.

'Hurry up,' Dave groused from behind me. Impatiently, he pushed me down the last two steps. I stumbled but caught myself.

'Don't you dare touch her,' Emory snarled.

'Jinx!' came an alarmed shout. It was a voice I recognised.

I swung towards the sound and my mouth dropped open a little.

Chained to the cellar wall was Stone.

CHAPTER 25

'STONE?' I SAID, bemused.

'What the hell are you doing here?' he demanded.

'You can talk later when I'm not here to listen to your moaning,' Dave interrupted. 'Dragon, come here.'

'I wouldn't talk that way to the Prime Elite, if I were you,' I advised him.

Dave shrugged. 'You'll all be dead soon, sweetheart. The boss has called in one of his pet griffins. You're going to be sliced and diced very soon.' He pushed Emory to the wall next to Stone and cuffed his feet. The ankle restraints also glowed blue.

'You next,' he instructed me. I moved towards Stone and Emory before he could push me again. 'Not there,' Dave said impatiently. 'Here.' He put me on the wall opposite them and fastened on the separate ankle restraints. And these ones didn't gleam. I guess they were just your regular type of shackle.

'Can you at least take off my handcuffs?' I asked. 'My shoulders are really aching.'

He rolled his eyes. 'No deal, babe. The boss will be in to see you soon with your hound, and then it's curtains. At least he's hired in again. Lucky you.'

'You keep talking about the boss. You told me you didn't know him?'

Dave frowned at me; he couldn't remember our conversation because I'd cleared his mind, and he was trying to work out how I knew that. After a moment's pause, he must have decided what the heck. 'It turns out I do know the boss. I thought he was a cog, like me. Turns out he's the biggest cog of all. He's the man behind every order.'

Dave's tone was bordering on worshipful. He was beyond impressed with the boss-man having feigned a lowly position for so long, pulling the strings behind the curtain. Having dropped that bombshell, he climbed back up the stairs and the door clanged shut above us.

I took a moment to look around. The dank room was cold and lit by a single bulb hanging forlornly from the low ceiling. There were no windows and no furnishings. The room could really do with some homey touches.

'What on earth are you doing here?' Stone asked again, sounding annoyed.

I glared at him. 'What am I doing here? What are *you* doing here? You disappeared without so much as a "cheers, thanks for hanging with me, Jinx!"'

'I was sent undercover. I didn't have time for farewells. You were passed out, if you remember.'

Emory snorted. 'Such a gentleman, leaving while you were unconscious.'

Stone glowered at him. 'This is none of your business, Prime.'

'On the contrary. The woman that I'm dating is very much my business.'

I opened my mouth to say we weren't dating but closed it again. I'd spent several hours kissing Emory; even if I wasn't dating him, I was certainly doing something with him.

Stone's expression was a little hurt. 'You're dating a creature? A dragon? I thought we had something, Jinx.'

'So did I,' I admitted. 'But it transpired that you'd compelled me to trust you. Everything we had was based on bullshit.'

Stone looked guilty then shook his head. 'It was real. Everything between us was real. I didn't know you when I compelled you – you were just someone I needed to work with. I realise it probably crossed a line with you, but it was the right thing to do at the time.'

'But you didn't stop the compulsion,' I pointed out. 'It was still there when Mrs H's magic undid it.'

'I wanted to undo it, but I'd have had to take you to a witch or a seer to get it removed, and we just didn't have time for that. Hes's life was on the line. Anyway, I knew you'd come to trust me naturally, so what difference did it make?'

'Everything,' I snarled. 'You don't compel people to trust you, you earn their trust. You show that you're worthy of it.'

'Jinx, we were in a hurry and we needed to work well together. We're both lone wolves and we needed a push to get the dynamic started. But once it was there, that was all us.' He was sincere; his eyes were entreating me to believe him.

Without my radar, I couldn't tell whether that was the truth or a lie. I shook my head at him. 'You should never have compelled me. Never. I can't forgive you that.'

'I don't accept that. I need to earn your trust? Fine, then I'll earn it every day until I've got it back.'

'That's going to take a long time,' I said flatly. It takes a long while for me to trust anyone; it takes even longer for me to forgive someone who lets me down.

'You're worth it,' Stone promised. Then he cut his eyes to Emory. 'So back off.'

Emory laughed. 'Afraid of some competition Stone?'

'You're not competition,' Stone sneered. You were a placeholder until I was back.'

I felt affronted. 'He most certainly was not! What kind of girl do you think I am?'

'It's not you,' Stone assured me. 'It's him. Dragons are so used to getting their own way, buying their way into every vote.' His voice was vitriolic in a way I'd never heard before.

'I'm not a girl to be bought,' I said firmly.

'Your apology isn't going so well,' Emory said to Stone, a tad gleefully. 'In fact, I can't help but notice you haven't apologised at all to Jessica.'

'Jessica, is it?' Stone eyes were incandescent with fury.

I cleared my throat. 'He's right, you know. Where's my apology?'

Stone turned to me. 'I'm sorry for compelling you, but it was for the greater good.'

My eyes narrowed. 'For future reference, an apology that has a "but" in it is a pretty shitty one.'

He met my eyes. 'I'm sorry,' he said simply.

I waited for my heart to soften but it didn't. Sometimes my capacity to hold a grudge surprises even me. Nevertheless, I went through the motions. 'I accept your apology.'

Stone smiled slowly. 'Forgive me?'

'Don't put the cart before the horse,' Emory advised cheerfully.

'Stop interfering,' Stone snapped. 'This has nothing to do with you.'

'*Our* disagreement has nothing to do with Emory,' I agreed, 'but I *am* dating him.' Kind of. 'Whatever was between us, you need to let it go. Maybe, with time, we can be friends.'

'I don't want to be a friend,' Stone protested. 'I want to marry you.'

If I hadn't been leaning against a wall, I would have fallen over. 'What? Are you kidding me? We spent like … three days together!'

'You're coming on too strong,' Emory advised Stone.

Stone roared, 'Will you shut the hell up?'

'I'm enjoying myself.' Emory shrugged.

'Unless it escaped your notice, we're being held prisoner,' Stone bit out. 'This is not the time to be having a lark.'

'You're right,' I interrupted before the situation could degrade further. 'Tell us what you're doing here.'

Stone clenched his jaw and continued to glare at Emory then let out a sharp breath and turned to me. 'I was placed undercover. We had an informant in the cartel. Unfortunately, he was terminated before I could bed in, and I got rooted out as well. I've been a guest here for just over a week. I expect they're trying to get the Connection to ransom me.'

'Will they?' I asked, genuinely curious.

'No, but my father will.' Actually, Stone didn't seem too worried about his current state, and I could see why. Although he was chained up, his clothes looked fresh, and he didn't smell. His face was clean shaven. He was a prisoner, but a well-looked-after prisoner.

'Your informant was Reggie Evergreen?'

Stone nodded, his eyes curious.

'I was hired to find his killer,' I said.

Stone smiled admiringly. 'And here you are. You've got great instincts.'

'Suck up,' Emory coughed.

That almost made me laugh, although I tried to throw Emory a quelling glance. He winked back at me. I obviously needed to work on my quelling glances.

I knew Emory was getting a kick out of winding up Stone, but I was also pretty sure he was trying to keep my spirits up. I appreciated the thought, but I could do that for myself. Now I knew what was going on, it was time to work on getting free. I was hoping Nate was en route with a few cohorts of vampyrs, but for all I knew, he was still in an airport somewhere. I had to rely on myself to get out of here.

My silk dress had the pocket on the right, and its enticing slit up the left-hand side. The dress was full skirted and when we had danced it had flared out as we'd twirled. I couldn't do a full twirl with my ankles restrained, but my hips had a lot of free movement. I started to turn my hips left and right, getting the skirt of my dress to sway. I put a little more sharpness in the movement, and as the material moved to the right, I caught it behind my back.

I carefully inched both hands down the skirt until the pocket was twisted along my back. I stepped forwards as far as I could and arched backwards; that allowed me some extra movement to reach into my dress pocket. I touched Glimmer first and my lock-picking set second.

Glimmer was my backup, but I didn't want to be holding it when the big boss came down the stairs. There was no need to give him a heads up that his goons hadn't searched me; Dave obviously wasn't the sharpest crayon in the box. My lock-pick set had a small catch on the top to keep it closed. I pulled it open easily and felt around until I pulled out a rake. A weak lock can be raked without any pressure and I felt a triumphant grin spread across my face as the handcuffs clicked open. My magic surged back into me. I'd missed it; in only a few short weeks, it had become an essential part of my being.

The smile was wiped off my face as the door clanged open. I kept my hands behind my back and tried to drop the rake back into my pocket. The cuffs were still on, albeit unfastened, so I didn't want to make any sudden moves and inadvertently make them clatter to the floor now we had an audience.

Down the narrow stairs came Ronan.

Everything slid into place. The only ones who had known about the incident with the dryad kid were Reggie and Ronan. Joyce had told Reggie I was a truth seeker and he'd worded his answers to all of my questions oh so carefully. It had set off alarm bells but not quickly enough. And the message on Reggie's computer, '*Dear R – I can't keep doing this. I love you. I'm sorry.*' It hadn't been a message *to* Reggie, but a message *from* Reggie to

Ronan: Ronan the piper, his best friend who could control unicorns.

I groaned. Why was everything always clear as day after the fact? Then I pulled myself together. It wasn't game over.

'Ronan,' I greeted him casually. He was followed by Dave and they both had triangles on their heads. They were in the Other with full access to their magic, though I realised I had no idea what Dave's magic was.

'Jinx,' Ronan replied equally casually.

'Nice wordsmithing with some of the questions I asked you,' I complimented him.

His smile didn't reach his eyes. 'Why thank you.'

'You killed Reggie, your best friend. You grew up together. You comforted his wife!'

'I didn't kill him myself – I couldn't have done that. But yes, I ordered his death. One of the griffins carried out my orders, but I still don't know which one. That's good, because I'd be tempted to murder the assassin for killing my best friend. Reggie's death was heart-breaking, but it had to be done because he killed Miller. I can't let anyone go around killing members of my team; it sends out the wrong message. And then ... Stone. Reggie brought the wrong inspector into my business and I had to shut down the whole operation. We'll have to relocate and start over. It is going to cost me millions, all because Reggie had an attack of conscience. Drugs are drugs.

People always want them, and people like me will always provide them.'

Ronan sighed. 'Reggie was a fool. He was my best friend, and I loved him, but his death was necessary. Don't worry, I'll take good care of his wife and children. Drugs are just a small part of what I'm doing here. This is bigger than me and Reggie. I'm building an empire, for the good of the human race.'

He sneered at Emory. 'For too long the pipers have been side-lined and looked down on, but with a boost to our powers we can control even the strongest of the creatures. At their hearts, they're still beasts.' The scary thing was that every word he spoke was true. He believed it all, utterly.

'I'll show you.' Ronan gave a long whistle and down the narrow staircase came a familiar figure.

'Gato!' I cried. He was in stealth mode and he looked like an ordinary Great Dane.

Roman whistled again and Gato began to grow into his Battle Cat shape.

I tried again. 'Gato?' His head swung towards me but there was no recognition in his eyes. 'Pup?'

Roman smirked. 'I told you I wanted my own hell hound. He was easier to draw under than I expected. Something had already weakened him but we'll soon get him into shape. He trotted quite happily out of the house when he was piped.' Roman ran his hands over Gato's obsidian spikes. 'I wonder what drugs we could make out of these.'

'Don't you dare touch him!' I snarled.

'Don't worry, I'm not going to let him hurt you, Jinx. My very own hell hound and my very own truth seeker. Because if you don't tell me what I need to know, then your hound will suffer the consequences. Your companions, however, are a different story.' Ronan paused then ordered Gato, 'Kill Stone.' He whistled a happy little trill that didn't sound like an order to kill someone.

'My father will ransom me,' Stone growled. 'You're making a mistake.'

'Gato, no!' I shouted.

Gato ignored me and started to stalk forwards. I frowned. I'd seen him in battle, and this wasn't it. I felt a glimmer of hope. While all eyes were on Gato, I let my cuffs drop, the material of my skirt muffling the sound. I reached with my free hand to my pocket, to Glimmer.

My legs were still manacled. Although Ronan was close to me, I wasn't sure if he was close enough. He'd have to be.

'What are you waiting for?' Ronan shouted to Gato. 'Kill Stone.'

Gato leapt abruptly but to the side, not forwards, and took down Dave with his jaws. Dave didn't even manage to scream as his blood painted the walls.

I made my move at the same time, not for myself but

for Emory and Stone. Glimmer was in my hand and it was singing. Without conscious thought or choice, I bent and cut effortlessly through the manacles securing my right foot. I pivoted; with the extra reach I could get to Ronan.

Glimmer sliced through his throat without hesitation or remorse. It sang with death as Ronan fell, his life's blood pouring out of his throat.

CHAPTER 26

I STARED AT my blood-soaked hands and shakily put Glimmer back in my pocket. Even tucked away, I could hear its song. It was triumphant, delighted to have been used once more.

With Ronan and Dave dead we were out of the woods but not home free. We needed to get out, and fast. If Ronan had the means to own a freaking castle, he was bound to have a small army of minions.

My phone rang in my pocket.

'Dave did a shit job of patting you down,' Stone commented.

'He didn't even think of it. Dresses don't usually have pockets. Dave wasn't the best underling.' I answered the phone.

It was Mo. 'Jinx. The companies you asked about, they're both owned by a man called Ronan Fallows.'

'Thanks,' I said drily.

'Am I calling at a bad time?'

'No, you did good. Thanks, Mo.'

'Nothing on the other project yet, but I'm on it. I've

found a few hints but they keep disappearing like smoke. I'll find him,' Mo promised. I was glad he hadn't named Bastion; Emory's sensitive hearing would probably have picked that up. He wouldn't be keen on me pursuing the deadly assassin by myself.

'I'm betting on it. Thanks.' I hung up. I sent Emory an amused look. 'Flight Fallow was owned by Ronan Fallows, apparently.'

'It would have been handy to have that call half an hour ago.'

'Yeah,' I agreed, 'then we could have aborted Operation Masked Ball.'

'True,' said Emory. 'But I enjoyed the drive here, so it was worth it.'

My skin warmed. 'Worth getting kidnapped and cuffed to a wall without your magic?'

'Definitely. I wouldn't want to be anywhere else.'

'Now who's sickening?' Stone muttered.

I rolled my eyes. 'Enough.' I knelt down and used Glimmer to slice through my other manacle before freeing the men.

Suddenly there was a loud shriek, and the door above us burst open once more. A griffin flew down the stairs and landed neatly next to Gato. Gato was unfazed.

'Shirdal,' Emory greeted the griffin calmly.

'I came to rescue you,' the griffin harrumphed, 'and you don't need me. Well, that's disappointing, let me tell you.' He turned to me. 'Hello, sweetheart. Are you okay?'

'I'm fine, thank you, Shirdal.'

Stone was making strangling noises. 'You've met Shirdal, harbinger of death?'

'So have you,' I pointed out. 'Shirdal this is Inspector Stone of the Connection.'

Shirdal inclined his head. 'Your reputation precedes you, inspector.'

'As does yours,' Stone said darkly.

'Play nicely,' I chastened. 'He's here to help.'

'Let's get out of here,' Emory suggested.

Shirdal led the way. When we reached the top of the stairs, we could hear the screaming. We started moving across the courtyard. The bodies of what I assumed were Ronan's men were littered everywhere in the moonlight.

'Ah,' said Emory, giving the griffin a pat in commiseration. 'Never mind, Shirdal. Your count can start from scratch again.'

'Yes,' Shirdal agreed mournfully. 'Zero.'

My mind struggled to make sense of the destruction that I could see. I couldn't even begin to count the bodies. There was an arm here, a leg there. I could see why Stone hadn't been warm and fuzzy with Shirdal. Stone was a representative of law and order, and this was as far as you could get from that.

Shirdal was watching me with golden eyes. 'Death and maiming.' He sighed. 'No torture though, so I'm still on the upswing.' He sounded a little hopeful.

Someone let out a battle cry from the shadows. He was a tall, muscle-bound man, and he was wielding a sword like it was a normal accessory. He roared towards Shirdal, blade raised. Shirdal flung his wings out effortlessly and brought them down. Wafts of air washed over me as he raised himself up, drew level to his opponent and waited.

With a shout, the man drew back his sword and charged. Shirdal flew around fluidly, never quite where I expected him to be. His attacker flung the sword towards him, and Shirdal easily stopped the swing of the blade with his claws.

I cried out and stepped forwards, expecting Shirdal to lose one of his claws but he didn't. Emory touched my wrist, stilling me. 'He'll be fine. Just give him space.'

My heart was in my throat. I felt like we should be helping Shirdal, but the two warriors were locked in battle, and it would be wrong to interfere. On and on the fight went, clash and swish as sword and claws collided.

Emory called out, 'Enough. Stop toying with him.'

Shirdal gave a little nod, and his attack changed. Gone were his languid movements; instead he ripped the sword out of his opponent's hand with his beak and used his talons to rip open his rival's throat. It was over in a second. I realised then that Shirdal had been toying with his opponent all along. As the bodies strewn about the castle indicated, when Shirdal meant business his business was death.

The griffin landed near me, his golden eyes sorrowful, expecting me to recoil in horror now I had seen what he could do. Part of me wanted to. My parents had been killed by a griffin, killed in a violent way much like the souls around us. But I had forgiven Stone when he had beheaded a vampyr in front of me and this was no different. Shirdal had been attacked and he had defended himself – and us. I couldn't think badly of him for that.

I gave his head a pat. 'Thank you for coming to rescue us. And it's safe to say you've put a stop to the drug cartel. Their ranks are somewhat decimated. I think this one is still in your plus column.'

Obviously my sense of morality was flexible. The drug manufacturers and distributors had known what they were getting into, and they'd been maiming and torturing unicorns to make a quick buck. And the drugs they sold had killed; they had killed Conrad and nearly killed Mererid. I was struggling to work up any sympathy for the corpses littered around. Maybe tonight I'd see their faces in my nightmares, but I was still grateful for Shirdal coming to help us and I wasn't going to make him feel bad about it. He was a griffin; death was their thing, and apparently they were damned good at it.

Gato came up to me and gave me a big lick. 'You scared me!' I told him. 'Pretending to be under Ronan's thrall – honestly, I was very upset. You shouldn't have gone with him.' Gato gave me another lick; I got the feeling he was ignoring my chastisements.

'He's bonded to you,' Emory pointed out, 'and the bond supersedes everything, even a piper. It's one of the reasons a hound will bond, giving them protection from a pipers call. For whatever reason, Gato chose to come with Ronan willingly.'

I glared. 'You couldn't have mentioned this before?'

He threw an arm around me and kissed my forehead. 'Didn't want to ruin Gato's big reveal.'

I heard the tell-tale whomping of an approaching helicopter. Actually, a few helicopters. 'That'll be the brethren,' Emory said.

'You sent out an SOS too?' I asked.

He raised an eyebrow. 'Who did you send an SOS to?'

'To me.' Nate stepped out of the shadows with Verona and a few others I recognised.

I gave them a wave. 'Hi, guys. Thanks for coming.'

Verona looked around, her eyes gleaming with something I was afraid to label as lust. 'Looks like we missed the party. You guys get all the fun.'

'Sorry,' I said. 'Next time there's a massacre I'll call earlier.'

Verona eyed my blood-spattered gown. 'Now *that* is a sexy dress.'

I sighed as I looked down. Bloodstains are a bitch to

get out of silk.

Nate stepped forwards, and I felt his presence like another limb. For eight weeks we'd been apart while he railed against our bond, and for eight weeks his absence had been like an itch in my brain that I couldn't scratch, a constant irritation. He must have felt it too because he stepped forwards, hugged me and let out a soft sigh.

I hugged him back. I felt better for having him there. I knew he would never hurt me; all he wanted was to see me safe. My personal bodyguard. The itch settled.

Nate stepped back. 'I leave you for a few weeks and this happens.' He gestured to all of the bodies. 'If you wanted to hang out, you should have just called. We don't need a bloodbath every time.'

I grinned at him. 'I'm glad you're back. Hey, how come you guys could come in? It's Ronan's home, right? Don't you need to be invited?'

Nate grinned. 'Commercial property,' he explained. 'We entered through the spa.'

'Nice. Nate, this is Emory, the Prime Elite.'

I immediately felt Nate's rising prejudice and countered it. 'I'm dating him, so you can't be rude.'

He frowned and scrubbed a hand through his hair. 'He's a dragon, though. My sworn enemy.'

'Sure, but he's very nice so...' I trailed off. I had a command bond over Nate. I could order him to be nice, and I could even order him to like Emory, but I was careful to do neither.

Nate gave me a small smile. He knew it too. He looked at Emory for a long moment, his emotions carefully banked. Finally, he held out his hand. 'A friend of Jinx's is always welcome,' he said tightly. 'Just give me a few weeks to get used to it.' I could feel the effort it took to curb his disdain, and I appreciated it.

Emory raised an eyebrow and looked at Nate's outstretched hand. He looked at me, back to Nate, then he took Nate's hand.

CHAPTER 27

THE BRETHREN CAME shortly after the vampyrs. They'd called in the Connection and Elvira arrived with her underlings soon afterwards. She glared at me, which softened a little as I scooched closer to Emory. Stone was all hers if he wanted her – and that was the main issue between them. He'd told me once that he could never love Elvira; he hadn't known then that he was lying to himself.

Emory's dragon, Fabian, was gone from the castle before the Connection arrived. He had slipped away before the brethren could approach him. A few likeminded guests had also gone, including the witch I'd thought might be Amber's rogue. Nor was there any sign of Ronan's 'pet' griffin. When Shirdal promised he'd look into the griffin's identity for me, it rang as a truth. When he promised he'd tell me the result of his investigations, it rang as a lie.

I wasn't sure how I felt about that. Ultimately Ronan was the one responsible for Conrad and Reggie's deaths. That wasn't a conversation I was looking forward to having with Joyce; she'd lost her husband and now she'd lost Ronan. I suspected she'd still mourn for him, for the man he'd once been, the best man at their wedding. But I doubted Joyce would care about the name of the assassin, a hired killer, a griffin from the assassins' guild. If it hadn't been him – or her – then it would have been another one. For now, I could live with Shirdal not telling me the name.

The guests who hadn't snuck away had a lot of explaining to do. Most of them claimed ignorance of the goings-on and declared that they were there for a charity ball, nothing more. I opened my mouth to volunteer my truth-seeking abilities but closed it again as I remembered how Ronan had wanted to use me.

Across the courtyard Stone nodded at me. I grimaced but sent him a shrug. Not much I could do here. The Connection were trying to identify the bodies and cordoning off the scene. There was a fair amount of bitching about the scattered limbs – Shirdal had made a mess.

I heard Stone telling Elvira that there was a laboratory beneath the castle, presumably where they'd manufactured the drugs, though Dave had said the farm was the centre of it all. Elvira had also suspected the farm was a front; as soon as she got the call to come to Rithean Castle, she'd ordered a similar raid on it. With two decisive strikes and the death of Ronan, the cartel had been delivered a sizeable blow, though only time would tell if it was crippling.

Ronan had kept encrypted records which the Connection were confiscating to decode. Hopefully they would lead them to any other players who were still at large. There was reference within the files to a second laboratory but the location remained hidden for now.

Stone told me I didn't need to give a statement and I could go home. It was odd, but after camping there for the best part of a week home felt like Lucy's. I guess I hadn't been in Liverpool long enough for it to settle. I'd been raised in the Home Counties and it would take a while before I accepted Merseyside as home.

I called Lucy. She was beside herself with worry, telling me through tears that Gato had gone out to the front garden and disappeared. I reassured her that he'd found his way to me, but I was scant on the details. She was too relieved to press me on it. Lucy said she intended to drink some wine and to see James. I couldn't blame her.

'Where to?' Emory asked.

James was going to Lucy's, so... 'Home, I guess.' I rattled off my new address on the Wirral and Emory repeated it to his pilot, Chris. Gato would get his helicopter ride after all.

I was exhausted. The adrenaline firing through me had long since faded, leaving me worn and tired. I let out a massive yawn and leaned on Emory's shoulder. He helped me into the helicopter and secured my harness.

He held out an animal harness to Gato, who let out a low growl of discontent. Emory dropped it. 'Suit yourself,' he muttered. 'Don't complain to me if you get thrown about.'

Gato gave him a superior look, turned three times and settled down on the floor.

Emory toggled the helicopter pilot and we set off. I closed my eyes, imagining the beach and the waves, shutting away the images of the devastation Shirdal had wrought.

When Emory gently woke me as we set down near my house, I rubbed my eyes and tried to wake up. 'I'll walk you to your door,' he said as he helped me out of the helicopter. He turned to the pilot. 'Ten minutes,' he ordered.

The pilot nodded and turned off the motor. Gato leapt down out of the helicopter, wagging his tail enthusiastically.

'You liked that ride, boy?' I asked.

He barked an affirmative, jumping around in enthusiasm. I smiled; I love that dog. 'Hush now, no barking. It's late.' It was: it was nearly 1 a.m. I was glad Emory had offered his arm; I was one hundred percent leaning on him, maybe twenty percent because I needed to, and eighty percent because I wanted to.

We reached the door of my modest semi-detached

house. 'This is me,' I said. Emory nodded and pulled me into a warm hug. He smelled great but, despite that, not one hormone responded. I was way beyond lust.

He kissed me on my forehead. 'Are you okay? Do you need help showering?'

I gave him a light push. 'I'm tired, not dead. I'll manage.'

'Okay.' He leaned in and softly brushed my lips with his. 'I've got to go and locate Fabian. And there's something else I need to finalise. I'll be back, but probably not tomorrow. I'm not doing a Stone. I'll be in touch.'

'And you definitely haven't compelled me or interfered with my mind in any way.' I said it as a statement, but we both know there was a little insecurity creeping in.

'I definitely haven't compelled or interfered with your mind in any way,' he stated. *True.* It was nice to have my radar back.

'Thanks,' I said. And he knew what I was thanking him for.

He laughed. 'Any time. You're a really fun date.'

'We need to work on your definition of fun.'

'There was fine dining,' he pointed out.

'Pasta in a limo,' I countered.

'There was passion,' he continued like I hadn't spoken. 'Dancing, drinks.'

'There was murder, mayhem and mutilation.'

'As I said, fun.' He brushed his thumb down my cheek. 'In you go. You're asleep on your feet. Gato, look after her.'

Gato barked. 'Shhh,' I said as I opened the front door.

Hes was in the hallway. 'Hey, Jinx.' Her eyes widened as she took in my bloodstained gown. 'Are you okay?'

'Yeah. I just went on a date with a dragon.'

She blinked. 'Sure.'

'You have a roomie?' Emory queried.

'Sometimes. Hester this is Emory. Emory this is Hester. Hes is new to the Other, like me.'

'Welcome, Hester.' Emory smiled. 'Can you be a good friend and help Jinx to the shower?'

'Of course,' Hester replied, still staring.

I harrumphed. 'I don't need a body attendant.'

Emory gave me a slow smile. 'I'll attend to your body any time you need.' It should have sounded sleazy but nothing about Emory was sleazy and I blushed again.

'Right. Good to know,' I said. 'You'd better go. You're keeping your pilot waiting.'

'Pilot?' Hester asked.

'Helicopter,' Emory explained.

'Sure,' Hester repeated, as if it were normal. Maybe it was for her; she'd grown up rich too.

Emory took my hand, bowed over it and kissed it. 'Sleep well, Jessica Sharp. I'll be in touch.' As he walked away, he looked back and smiled when he saw I was still watching. I gave him a wave, and his smile widened.

I shut the door when he was out of sight and went up to the bathroom. 'I don't need help to shower,' I said to Hes. 'But can you unzip me?'

She unfastened the dress, and I stepped out of it, letting it pool to the floor. 'Can you bin it?' I asked. 'There's no saving that silk.'

Hes gathered it up in her arms as I stripped down and got in the shower. Only when I was standing under the water did I remember I was still wearing Emory's emerald pendant.

I dried my body perfunctorily and dressed in pyjamas. I was too tired to dry my hair.

'Come here,' Hes ordered. I followed her into my spare room, her room when she wanted it. She sat me down and dried my hair for me then helped me back up. I slid into bed and Gato climbed in next to me.

'Night,' Hes called as she clicked off the light.

'Night, Hes. Thanks.'

As I snuggled down, I reflected how strange it was to have so many people in my life that seemed to care for me. I was in danger of getting friends. I think the feeling that I had was happy.

I REALLY WAS exhausted and I didn't wake up until a long

time later. Hes and I had a lazy day; she bunked off lectures, and I put my 'out of office' on to field any emails. We had a *Friends* marathon, ate pizza and drank a bottle of wine between us.

It made me miss Lucy and wish we'd said goodbye properly. Impulsively I texted her to say I'd be back down to her house tomorrow to pick up my stuff and my car. And it was a great excuse to hang out. I got an enthusiastic response; she was tired from her night with James, wink-wink, but she would get a good sleep tonight so we could hang out. I can always count on Lucy.

Later, Hes got a call from some uni friends and took a taxi back to halls. I was a little tipsy, but other than that I was fine. I switched on some more trashy TV and had just settled down when I got a text from Mo: *Your latest project is proving elusive – this is going to take some time … and expense.*

My heart was pounding a little as I replied: *Take as long as you need; no expense spared. Find him.*

He's a ghost, was Mo's instant reply. *But when he makes a mistake, I'll find him.*

I blew out a breath and called for Gato. I switched off the TV. I needed a walk to clear my head. My happy tipsiness was gone, and all I was left with was anger. The alcohol had loosened my emotions. Thinking of Bastion, the assassin who had literally torn my parents apart, made my vision go red. I needed to calm down.

This chase wasn't a sprint, it was a marathon. Sooner or later Bastion would slip up, and Mo would get me the lead I needed. I did some breathing exercises my dad had taught me, and Gato and I went for a walk around the block.

The night air helped kiss away the last vestiges of my rage. I felt calm and centred once more when I reached my driveway. Emory, dressed impeccably as ever, was leaning against my front door.

I gave him a huge smile, which he didn't return. Mine faded. 'Emory?'

'Let's go in,' he suggested, still solemn.

Oh man, he was breaking up with me. We'd only had one date and a few kisses. He'd seemed fine last night, so what had changed in twenty-four hours? I wracked my brain and came up blank. Old insecurities reared their heads. Who was I kidding? I wasn't good enough for him.

I led him into the lounge, sat on my couch and gathered a blanket around me. 'What's up?' I asked tightly.

Emory sighed. 'There isn't an easy way to say this, so I'm just going to come out with it. You know how tired Lucy was? And then how ill Gato was?'

I frowned; this wasn't where I thought this conversation was going. 'Yeah, so?'

'I've seen something similar before. I've done some digging. Lucy's boyfriend, James, is an incubus. Gato was trying to save her.'

Save Lucy? 'What? What are you talking about?'

'Gato was giving Lucy his energy, trying to give back what had been stolen. James has broken the Verdict. Under its terms, he's only allowed to feed on one human once. From what I can gather, he's been with Lucy four times, maybe five.'

'I don't understand,' I said blankly.

'Jinx, I'm sorry.' He ran a hand through his dark hair. His green eyes met mine, and the compassion and sympathy were my undoing.

'Just say it,' I whispered, my heart thundering, my gut twisting.

He took my hand. 'I'm so sorry, Jinx. There's nothing we can do. Lucy is dying.' *True.*

My world imploded.

BOOK 3 – GLIMMER OF DEATH

Don't panic! Despite that cheeky hook...book 3 is coming very very soon. In fact it is available for pre-order now! Book 4 will also follow in rapid succession and in a few months you will have a complete series to read again and again. You're welcome.

ACKNOWLEDGEMENTS

Thank you so much to my Beta and ARC team who have been so wonderful about supporting me. You have all given me so much time and enthusiasm, it's been humbling. You guys rock!

Thanks to my sisters, who have beta read all of my books and told me that they loved them. We've been through quite the rough patch but they've helped me through it all. Love you.

Finally, thanks to all of you, my readers. You make everything possible. Thanks for following me down the rabbit hole.

ABOUT THE AUTHOR

Heather is an urban fantasy writer and mum. She was born and raised near Windsor, which gave her the misguided impression that she was close to royalty in some way. She is not, though she once she got a letter from the Queen's lady-in-waiting.

Heather went to university in Liverpool, where she took up skydiving and met her future husband. When she's not running around after her children, she's plotting her next book and daydreaming about vampyrs, dragons and kick-ass heroines.

Heather is a book lover who grew up reading Brian Jacques and Anne McCaffrey. She loves to travel and once spent a month in Thailand. She vows to return.

Want to learn more about Heather? Subscribe to her newsletter for behind-the-scenes scoops, free bonus material and a cheeky peek into her world. Her subscribers will always get the heads-up about the best deals on her books.

Newsletter: heathergharris.com/subscribe
Follow her Facebook Page: facebook.com/Heather-G-Harris-Author-100432708741372
Instagram: instagram.com/heathergharrisauthor
Contact info: www.HeatherGHarris.com
HeatherGHarrisAuthor@gmail.com

REVIEWS

Reviews feed Heather's soul. She'd really appreciate it if you could take a few moments to review her book and say hello.